April Adventure

April Adventure

Adrian Manning

RavensYard Publishing, Ltd.
Fairfax County, Virginia USA

ISBN 0-9667883-5-4

Library of Congress Catalogue Card Number:
99-074502

This book is a work of fiction. The persons and events depicted
here are drawn from the imagination of the author. Any similarity
between the characters in this work and actual persons is unintend-
ed and purely coincidental.

Published by
RavensYard Publishing, Ltd.
P.O. Box 176
Oakton, Virginia 22124
USA
www.ravensyard.com

For Jennifer and Cindy.

Chapter One

Anna turned in the hard wagon seat for a last view of the bare wood house she was born in. She was anxious to get on with the trip from Lincoln County, North Carolina, down the bumpy red-clay road to the rail cars at Charlotte, but she felt a sadness leaving the small house her father had built. Anna had never been to Charlotte. She had never been more than six miles from her birthplace.

Mrs. Elizabeth Williams, Anna's mother, held the reins as the old mules pulled the creaking wagon. Anna had wanted to direct the team down the road but Mrs. Williams said, "I'll handle the team. You just keep us going in the right direction." Anna smiled. She didn't know what direction Charlotte was. But she wanted to get there, get on the cars and find her father.

Others in the wagon were a thin black woman known as "Settie Number One," and her daughter, "Settie Number Two," a girl about Anna's own age, 12. "Two" thought she was 12. She wasn't sure. The two black women sat on the wagon floor, hugging two carpetbags that contained all the Williams' clothing and worldly goods.

The county road was empty and dusty in the April heat. Anna felt the sun's warmth as it rose higher in the spring sky. The mules kicked up dust in the road. The women were leaving the farm that Henry Williams had bought in 1858, after he moved his wife and daughter to Lincoln County from Chester, South Carolina. Settie Number One and Two went to Lincoln with the Williams family. They had been owned by Henry's brother in Chester and sold to Henry, along with One's husband, Oscar.

After an hour on the bumpy road, Mrs. Williams halted the mule team in the shade of a tall tree by the Catawba River.

"Pass the water," she told Settie One. The black woman lifted a stone crock lid and raised a large spoon-shaped gourd and each took a long drink of the cool spring water. Settie One passed some biscuits that were wrapped in a red cotton cloth.

"We ought to be at Charlotte soon," Mrs. Williams said.

"Why haven't we seen anyone on the road, Mama?" Anna asked.

"There's no one left," her mother said softly. Anna saw pain in her mother's pale face. It was true there were few people left in the country this April 1865. First, Henry Williams went away with the Fourth North Carolina Regiment, to soldier with General Lee's army in Virginia. That was in 1863. Henry Williams wrote regularly to his wife and daughter but they hadn't heard from him in six months. Then Settie One's husband, Oscar, died of the night sweats the preceding winter. Without his help Mrs. Williams could not run the farm. It was too much for the women. Mrs. Williams decided that they would pack up and find her husband. Anna was thrilled; it was an adventure.

Settie One had fretted; Settie Two had wailed that the "patty-rollers" would get her. Mrs. Williams sat Two down and explained that the state patrollers who rode county roads in search of wandering slaves would not bother her as she would be with Mrs. Williams.

"Furthermore," Mrs. Williams said, "the patrollers have all gone to the army." Two was not entirely calmed, so great was her fear of the large men she heard about from her late father. "You never want to be on the road after dark," he had often warned her by the fire in their small cabin. "The patrollers will get you and hand you over at the county courthouse and then you will be gettin' a whippin' for being out on the road without a paper."

Two had never seen patrollers and she never had a paper. No slave in the country, her father also told her, would be given a paper. And no slave, he said, could read a paper. Slaves were not allowed to learn writing.

Anna and Two grinned at each other as they chewed their biscuits. Anna knew that there was no more food on the farm, one reason her mother had hitched the mules that morning. There was nothing on the farm to keep them there. They had no seed for the spring planting. The country had lost its men. Families had to fend for themselves.

Elizabeth sipped from the gourd and coughed. Anna saw her mother's cheeks redden.

"The cars will get us to Raleigh, where we'll stay with my sister," Mrs. Williams said. "From there we will find Mr. Williams…"

An hour later they rolled into a dusty crossroads outside Charlotte. Anna and Two stared down the wide main street and at the close built unpainted wood buildings. Soon they saw people in yards, women mostly, hanging wash. There were plenty of children in the yards but few men on the street and those were elderly.

Mrs. Williams turned the mule team onto a side street toward a faded sign that read: "Hostler-Blacksmith." She stopped the wagon and climbed down to enter the barn-like building that looked cool inside its inviting darkness. Anna smelled the pungent animal smell of the corral where two old horses stood in the sun.

Soon, Mrs. Williams returned with a white-haired old man who walked to the mules and looked them over. "Not young," he said.

"They're strong and healthy and worth what I'm asking," Mrs. Williams said. The old man motioned her into his building and Anna climbed down from the wagon seat.

"Now, don' you go roamin'," Settie·One said.

Anna shaded her eyes with her right hand and looked up the street. After hearing about Charlotte

Town from visitors to her farm, she was not impressed with the collection of unpainted wood buildings and shacks. Some of the holes in the road had water in them from the storm two nights before.

Anna had wandered to the corner to peer up the next road when she saw her mother return to the wagon. Anna ran to her. "Take the bags, Settie," Mrs. Williams said to the older black woman.

The two Setties clambered out of the wagon, dragging the large, dusty carpetbags. At the same time the old man came out and led the team and wagon inside his barn.

"He said there is a boardinghouse on Tryon Street, up a ways," Mrs. Williams said as they followed her down the grassy path by the road. Anna walked to her mother's right.

"He didn't give me what I had hoped. But it should be enough to get us to Raleigh on the cars," Mrs. Williams said.

"He paid me in coin and some Confederate bills. He told me they would accept the bills here in Charlotte…for the present."

The Tryon Street boardinghouse was a large three-story wood building set back from the street. They walked through the front-yard garden, where spring flowers had bloomed. Mrs. Williams knocked on the front door.

After a few moments the door opened and a large woman, dressed in a dark blue dress that covered her from shoulder to feet, asked, "Yes?"

Mrs. Williams explained they would need a room overnight, the servants, too. "They can sleep in the back with my nigrahs," the woman drawled. "Come in," she said to Mrs. Williams, while waving Settie One and Two around the rear of the house.

After the heat of the street, Anna found the house cool and dark. The tall woman led them into the parlor.

"It will be $3 for yawl," the woman said. Mrs. Williams reached for her skirt pocket and pulled out the money she had gotten from the hostler for the wagon and team. She put a $2 Confederate bill on the round table in the middle of the parlor. She added a dollar in old U.S. coin to it.

"Prefer if you had all coin," the woman said.

"Don't have it," Mrs. Williams said. The landlady shrugged. She led them upstairs to the third floor and a small room that contained a narrow bed and one chair.

"Girl can sleep on the floor," the landlady said. Anna suddenly missed her bed at home with its straw-filled mattress. She would make do.

"We'll make do," Mrs. Williams said. "Now, if you could give me directions to the depot, I'd be obliged…?" The landlady explained the depot was three streets away as Anna peered out the uncurtained window at the house across the wide street. It seemed deserted.

"Anna," her mother said, "find Settie and have her bring the bags here." Anna ran down the two flights of stairs to the rear of the building. She had never been in a house with as many rooms. She walked down a long, dark hallway that smelled of old food and people sweat. It was not the odors of her home, where Settie had done all the cooking in an outbuilding away from the main building. This house had its kitchen inside, a long room at the back of the building. Settie One and Two were in the kitchen talking with another black woman. Anna told One to bring the bags upstairs.

Anna met her mother in the hallway. "I'm going to the depot to see about tickets. You stay here and be mindful of the landlady." Anna noticed that her mother's cheeks were bright red.

A few minutes later Settie One descended the stairs to face Anna and Two. "Now, you all wash before we take our meal." Anna smiled at Two as she knew that both had large appetites and could eat at any time of day.

Anna and Two left the rear of the house by a steep set of wood stairs. They stood in a large yard that sloped away from them toward two privies set side by side at the far end of the yard. The garden filled most of the yard with the path in the middle to the privies. Anna saw that the landlady was raising spring greens and carrots. She smelled the pungent manure that was being shoveled around the plants by an old black man. Two walked up to him boldly.

"Do you live here?" Two asked.

The old man straightened. He wore a frayed straw hat, a tattered shirt and homespun pants that didn't reach his bare ankles. Anna saw him turn his head and spray a line of tobacco juice on the nearby plants.

"About twenty year now, young'un," he said. "If yawl gonna stand in my garden, I'm gonna put yawl to work with this here shovel," he said to Two. She laughed.

"We don't have to work. We travelin'."

Just then Anna heard a commotion from the front of the building, a clatter of wagons and animals. She and Two ran around to the front. They stood by a low holly bush and stared at the arrival of coaches and wagons, accompanied by a dozen dusty cavalrymen in mixed grey, brown and blue uniforms. They sat their horses as the party of a dozen men climbed from the coaches and wagons. The men were agitated, Anna saw, all seeming to be talking at once and most seemed angry. Anna saw that one tall, gaunt man did not join the hubbub. He walked alone to climb the stairs to the front door. He wore a black suit that was dusty on the arms and trousers near his boots.

Anna approached the soldiers dismounting from their thin horses.

"Where have you all come from?" Anna asked one young soldier closest to her.

"Richmond," he said, grinning at Anna. "Not all in one day." He waved to the tall man who now stood in the vestibule, speaking to the landlady. "That's President Davis," he said. Anna turned and stared in awe at the leader of the Confederacy. She had heard of Davis from her mother and father. But she had no idea what he looked like. Anna and Two followed the party into the house, where the landlady noticed them in the hallway and shooed them into the kitchen. The men entered the main parlor and sat themselves down.

In the kitchen Anna and Two found Settie One at a counter, cutting a large loaf of bread. She dipped the knife into a crock and slathered the bread with butter. "Real food," Anna said, as she and Two settled on a wood bench and savored the meal. Settie One gave each a tin cup of warm milk with the bread.

As the girls finished their meal they heard another commotion in the front of the house. Anna stood and walked down the hallway to find the landlady at the door, talking to two strange men.

"...and she fell to the floor at the depot," one man was saying.

"Carry her in here," the landlady said. The men went to a wagon and with the help of a few of the soldiers they carried Mrs. Williams up the stairs and into the house. "Mama," Anna said, seeing her mother's face, pale and unconscious.

"Girl," the landlady said to Anna, "go in the back and send that Amos for the doctor." The landlady turned to the soldiers holding Mrs. Williams. "You men carry her upstairs. Follow me."

Anna ran to the rear of the house, yelling, "Help, Settie, help!"

Chapter Two

The soldiers carried Mrs. Williams upstairs, their boots scraping the bare wood. The landlady, Settie One and Anna followed. The men put the woman on the bed, directed by the landlady. Then they shuffled their feet.

"Out, out," the landlady said. The men left. Anna heard them on the stairs. The landlady opened Mrs. Williams' blouse. Anna stared at her mother's face and closed eyes, and she shivered.

"I'll get some hot water," Settie One said. When her husband was dying at the farm it was all she could do for him.

"Get some cool water," the landlady said. Settie One went downstairs. The landlady turned to Anna.

"You—what's your name?" she asked, pointing at Anna. Anna told her.

"Take yourself downstairs and wait for the doctor, hear?" Anna nodded.

Anna stood on the front step for what seemed like hours until an old-fashioned, two-wheel carriage pulled by a large mule pulled up the street and stopped. The doctor climbed down. Anna saw he wore a black baggy suit and as he approached she noticed his smell and sweat-rimmed shirt. Anna heard the door open behind her and the landlady welcomed the doctor. "Upstairs, another boarder taken down," the landlady said.

Anna remained outside, idly watching the street, noticing the old black man turn the corner, walking with the aid of a crooked blackthorn stick. The old man did not hurry.

Anna climbed the stairs to her mother's room and arrived just behind the doctor and the landlady, who turned and closed the door in Anna's face.

Time slowed, as it does when there is worry in the house. Anna found the parlor and a comfortable chair in the cooler room. Hunching, Anna clasped her hands in prayer, as her mother had taught her. After a few minutes, Anna felt herself drowsing until she was awakened by loud voices in the hall.

"She can't be moved," the doctor said. "There's not much I can do for her. The one good thing is that it's not contagious."

"Can we send for her family to come get her?" the landlady asked.

"She told me she is on her way to find her husband in Virginia. She will have to stay here. There is no place else. She is too weak to be moved."

Anna entered the hall as the landlady walked the

doctor to the door. "I can't have a sick house here," the landlady said.

"I know you will do the right thing," the doctor said, nodding and heading toward his carriage.

Anna went to the kitchen to find Settie One with the other servants.

"Anna, girl, your mama sick bad," Settie One said. At that moment the landlady entered the kitchen,

"Mrs. Williams is serious ill, the doctor says," the landlady echoed Settie. "Can't be moved."

"What's wrong?" Anna asked. The landlady shook her head. "The hospital is closed; all the doctors went to the army. You," she said, pointing to Two, "take this basin out to the spring house and bring me clean water." The landlady bustled about the kitchen, preparing a wash cloth and towel. When Two returned with the water, the landlady handed Two the clothes and One, Two and Anna climbed the stairs.

They found Mrs. Williams in her petticoat and homespun blouse, pale and sweaty atop the rough bed. Settie One went to her side and began washing her face and neck. Anna and Two stood by the bed, afraid to speak. She saw, as if for the first time, her mother's frail body, sunken eyes and colorless skin as Settie worked the cloth across the woman's face and neck.

"Mama, what's wrong?" Anna whispered.

Mrs. Williams shook her head slowly. "We will have to wait here for your father. I'm afraid we can't go on," she said, attempting a smile. With effort, Mrs. Williams raised herself and reached in her blouse neck. "Here,

Anna. Watch over this." Mrs. Williams handed Anna folded papers. "I must sleep now. I'm very tired. I don't know what's bothering me…"

Later, in the kitchen with the old black man and the two younger women, Anna and Two watched as they prepared the evening meal of fried pork and garden greens. Despite her hurt, Anna was hungry.

"Food is getting short here in Charlotte Town," one woman told Settie One. "Why in the old days we had pork, beef and chickens as much as we wanted. This war…"

Anna walked to the back porch and sat down on the top step and pulled the papers her mother had given her from her skirt pocket. The papers were passage for two on the North Carolina Railroad and passage for two servants. The tickets on the cars to find her father. The papers also contained a few Confederate notes, amounting to $22. Anna put her head in her folded arms, close to tears.

She heard steps and looked up to see President Davis standing by her, still in his black suit.

"I understand your mother is ill. I'm very, very sorry," Davis said in a deep voice. Anna noticed that he held his head high and seemed to peer down at her.

"Yes, she's ill and now we can't go to Virginia…" Anna said.

Davis was silent a few moments. "Why do you want to go to Virginia?" he asked.

"To find my father," Anna replied. "He's with the army…"

"There is no army. It's over," Davis said with a shake of his head. "Have you heard from your father recently?"

"Not since January," Anna said. "Then it was only a short note brought us by a neighbor who was released because his wound would not heal. He died... My father is with the Fourth North Carolina..."

Davis shook his head again. "I know nothing of the troops these days. But you must not despair. We intend to regroup and carry on..." Davis patted Anna's head and re-entered the house.

Anna felt better for speaking with Mr. Davis. She never thought she would ever talk with the President of the Confederacy, the man who was leading the fight against Northern aggression, as her mother put it. Anna went back into the kitchen where the servants were cleaning the pots and pans. Anna walked through to the hallway, heading toward the stairs and her mother. She heard the men's voices from the hallway. They were in the main parlor.

"The children are now asking me for their fathers," Anna heard Davis say. She peered into the large room and saw Davis standing with three other men who had arrived with him.

"It's over, Mister President," a large, bearded man told Davis. "We gain nothing by running..."

Anna saw that Davis shuddered and exploded, "We are not running. We will take the battle from another front. The people are with us. The Yankees are tired of war. A few more campaigns and they will stop. We have

Joe Johnston here in Carolina…"

The large man stood his ground, Anna saw. "There aren't enough regiments left to field a brigade…The terms were signed by Lee." Anna saw that onlookers nodded agreement.

"No," Davis said. "Lee signed only for his army. He quit the field. I never thought I'd see the day that happened. We will continue from Texas, or failing that, from Mexico. We have come too far…"

One of the men took Davis by the arm and moved him to the other side of the room where they conversed quietly so that Anna could not overhear them.

Anna met Settie One on the stairs to her mother's room. Settie carried a plate. "She can't hold it down," the black woman said, shaking her head.

When Anna entered the room she saw that her mother was moving her head side to side and gasping. When she saw Anna, she tried to smile.

"We will have to wait here for Mr. Williams," she said. It was all she could say. Anna fell to her knees beside the bed.

"You will get better, Mama. I just know it. You can stay here until father comes…" She saw her mother slip into fitful sleep.

Anna found Two by the front door, peering out on the dark street. Anna opened the door for some air.

"Where you going?" Settie One asked from the darkened hallway. "Two, you stay in here, otherwise the 'pattyrollers' get you…"

"We don't have patrollers any more," the landlady

said from behind One. "They've all gone to the war…"

Anna remembered seeing the men on horseback that patrolled the county roads, seeking runaway Negroes. The Negroes feared being out at night because without papers they would be taken to the courthouse where they would be held in chains until their owner came for them. And that usually meant a whipping. Anna knew her father had never beaten his slaves. They worked the field and house and he said it made no sense to whip them to the point they could not work.

Henry Williams' farm could not be called a "plantation" because it was too small. He raised cotton on the hard, red land and garden vegetables for the table and for sale at the courthouse. That was 1863, the last good year. Henry Williams, Anna knew, had come up to the county from Chester, South Carolina, where all the good farming land was long since taken. Anna heard her father talk of the "plantation gentry" of the low country, where they farmed rice on huge plots and had hundreds of slaves to work the fields. She had never been out of the county before so she imagined what that life was like from her father's description of the country toward Charleston, where the war began.

Anna knew, however, that not all in her county were "Sechesh." Some of the upland people were still for the Union. They had no slaves and they looked with envy and anger at the secessionists from the eastern Carolinas.

Anna was a strong secessionist. She had heard her father say that no one should be able to tell another how to live. Slaves were, he said, his property.

When Henry Williams went to the army, Anna cried for three days. "He's just in the next state, Virginia," Mrs. Williams told her daughter. That calmed her; she had no idea what Virginia was like but it was Mr. Lee's home.

Anna's world was the rough-board, unpainted house in the clearing, a house with a loft for sleeping and a cook shack out back where Settie One prepared their meals. One and Two were considered house servants though they didn't sleep in the house. They slept in the cook shack where the large fireplace kept them warm in winter.

When it was apparent Mrs. Williams could not keep the farm going in the absence of her husband, she approached the church deacon at the courthouse. Anna was with her mother that March Sunday. The deacon was a withered old man who walked with a cane. "The needs are many and the resources are few," he told Mrs. Williams. "Go to your relatives."

Mrs. Williams said, "They are in Raleigh and I don't know what conditions they are in." The old man nodded and hobbled away. Anna later that day watched her mother write a note on the back of a scrap of wallpaper, close and sew it. A neighbor carried the letter to Charlotte, to be mailed to Raleigh. For weeks there was no reply.

Anna turned from the door and walked back to the parlor, where President Davis sat with his traveling companions. Though it was warm in the room, all wore their dark coats. Davis waved Anna to join him. She walked to his chair.

He smiled at her. One man nearby said, "We could ride to Columbia and find aid."

"You forget," Davis said, "Columbia is in the hands of the Federals. Are you proposing we surrender ourselves?" The other man stood quickly and protested.

"We could do that," Davis continued. "There would be some sense in it. They have Richmond and must be scouring the country looking for me. It would put a quick end to their hunt. But I think we will continue on our way."

Anna was surprised to hear President Davis talk surrender but she held her tongue. She realized how upset her mother would be if she spoke. The other men remained silent; Anna could see each was lost in thought. They were saying the war was over. The Confederacy had lost to the scoundrel Yankees. But Mr. Davis was alive and maybe something good would come of that.

The sallow-faced younger man spoke up about the routes to Alabama they would take the following day. "We will not have the cavalry escort, Mr. President. They have gone to join Joe Johnston where they can find him."

Anna was puzzled. The war was over but these men spoke of continuing the fighting. How could it be both? She slipped out of the room and went upstairs where she found Settie One washing her mother's face and chest. Anna could hear her mother's labored breathing across the room. It frightened her.

Later, sleeping on a rolled quilt on the floor, Anna decided what she must do the next day. She would go and find her father. He would know what to do to make her mother well.

Chapter Three

Anna awoke at the rooster's call. She saw her mother was still asleep. Anna went downstairs and out through the kitchen to the privy and then to the spring house to wash her face and hands. The cool water made her feel better. Settie One was in the kitchen when she returned to the house.

"I have boiled rice," Settie One said. Settie Two sat on the floor by the window. Her mother motioned to her. "When it's done, you take some to the mistress." Anna was not hungry.

Anna followed Two upstairs with the food. Anna helped her mother raise herself on the bed to take the rice. She was able to get a few mouthfuls before she shook her head. Anna felt her mother's brow. She was feverish and not entirely awake. "Mama, I'm going to find father for you," Anna said. Her mother nodded and slid down on the mattress.

As Anna and Two returned downstairs, Two asked her, "What do you mean you will find your father?"

Anna said, "I'll have to find him. It's the only way."

Back in the kitchen, Anna took some bread and butter from Settie One. "Settie," she said, "I'm going to find father."

Settie One looked at her closely. "Daughter, you have to wait till your mama is well."

"No!" Anna said. "I've decided that I have to go find father, to tell him what has happened." Anna turned to Two. "I'll take Two with me and as soon as we find father we'll bring him back here. You stay here with mother."

Settie One raised her hands to her face, as she usually did when she was nervous.

"I don't know, daughter. I can't tell you what to do but I don't think your mama wants you to leave…"

"Only for a short while," Anna said. She returned to her mother's room, where she took some clothing and put it in her small cotton bag. She had the railroad tickets in her skirt. She met Two in the downstairs hallway. "Are you prepared?" Anna asked.

"I don' have anything to take with me," Two said.

"That's all right, "Anna said. "We'll share. It won't take long, I'm sure." They left the house quietly. Anna knew that Settie One would speak with the landlady. Anna didn't want to talk with the landlady. The street was quiet in the early spring morning. The two girls walked down the grassy path to the main street and up it to the depot building. The depot was a one-story, red-brick building set in a neighborhood of one-story, unpainted wood houses.

A few carts and wagons stood in front of the depot. As the girls approached, a man walked a mule from the side of the building. They watched as he hitched the animal to a wagon. Anna noticed the man had a bedroll tied around his shoulder. She guessed he was a soldier though his clothes did not seem to be a uniform. They consisted of mismatched shirt and trousers held up with leather suspenders.

The girls walked to the depot's front door. Inside, the depot was dark after the early morning glare of the street. Dust specks glistened in the shafts of light that came through the high windows. As her eyes grew accustomed to the dark, Anna saw the room was filled with large wood benches, like a church. Men in various combinations of town and country clothing rested on the benches. Some had long-barrel muskets propped by their sides; most all were bearded and gaunt. Anna saw they resembled the horse soldiers who had accompanied President Davis the day before. Looking around she saw a tall beardless man standing at a tall desk, writing with a quill. The girls approached him but he didn't look up from his work.

"I would like to take the cars to Virginia," Anna said boldly. The man slowly put his pen in a glass cup at his elbow. He looked down at the girls with kindly eyes.

"Well, Miss," he said. "I'm not sure that the cars will go to Virginia or anywhere today…" He explained that the line was not clear, that the telegraph was out beyond Greensboro. "The last message I got by telegraph was to wait for the Federal authorities." He laughed and said,

"They didn't say when they were acomin'."

Anna turned away, unsure what to say. She hadn't counted on this. She saw a open door on the far side of the building to the tracks. The girls left the building and stood on the platform. Both stared in awe at the large black locomotive that bore gold lettering on its side that read "Rogers." Behind the locomotive were a tender filled with cut wood for the steam boiler and two small wood cars painted with faded red and white letters that read: "Carolina and Raleigh."

The cars, the girls saw, contained more lounging soldiers. Some rested elbows on the open window frames of the cars. Some smiled at the girls, white teeth flashing on dirty, bearded faces. Some slept on their arms. Some smoked corncob pipes. All wore the variety of mud-colored homespun that didn't look very military, at least not as military as the posters Anna recalled seeing portraying General Lee's valiant army.

Anna thought the soldiers looked like tramps she remembered seeing at her farm in the war's early years, when men roamed the region seeking work or, as her father more than once said, "avoiding the provost's soldiers." The provost rounded up ruffians and deserters, the way patrollers seized loose Negroes.

As the girls stared at the cars and their occupants, they heard a commotion behind them, inside the terminal. Anna peered in the doorway, Two behind her. She saw a large, bearded man dressed in a long, gray coat, wearing a wide-brim straw hat. There was all kinds of gold-colored materials on his sleeves. His booming voice was directed at the young man at the desk.

"These cars must get to Raleigh today," he said. "If this locomotive is not ready within the hour, " he yelled, "I will shoot all who have disobeyed my orders. Sergeant!" he boomed.

Anna saw a tall, sunburned older man stand slowly from one of the benches.

"Sir?" the tall man asked.

"Sergeant," the officer said, "Have your men load weapons and await my order…" The sergeant waved to the other men on the bench who sluggishly rose to their feet, clutching their muskets and reaching in the cotton sacks slung about their shoulders for shot and powder.

The young man paled when he saw this. "I will send for the engineer," he said quickly. No sooner said, Anna saw and a large man wearing a dark, dirty suit entered the depot. "Here he is now," the young man said in a high voice.

The officer repeated his instructions.

"Can't be done," the engineer said in a rough voice that Anna recognized as being from the mountains to the west. It was a voice rougher than the slurred speech of the lowland Carolinas.

"The Federals have all the rails blocked or tore up and we have orders to stand down," the engineer said.

"Get your locomotive steam up," the officer commanded.

"What are you to accomplish?" the engineer asked.

"Are you aware that General Lee surrendered. The war is over."

"Not for us," the officer said. "Or for Joe Johnston. We will fight on…" The officer drew his long-barrel pistol and pointed it at the engineer's chest. The engineer looked at the weapon.

"So, my choice is to be shot here or to be shot by the Federals…" The engineer shook his head wearily and walked by the girls to climb the iron ladder to his locomotive. From that perch he called to the officer, "I'll need men to feed wood to the boiler." The girls watched as the officer directed a few nearby men to climb the tender and pass wood to the engineer.

Anna approached the officer. "Sir, I would like to ride with you. See, I have passage," Anna said, holding up the tickets her mother had purchased.

The officer looked down at Anna, surprised. He took the tickets, reading them. "These tickets provide for two females and two servants to ride the cars. I'm afraid we are taking these cars on a military mission, miss."

Anna felt tears sting her eyes. "I am on a military mission, too," she said. "I aim to find my father with General Lee and return him safely to my mother."

The officer smiled at Anna. "Where is your mother?"

"She's at the boarding house. She was taken ill yesterday and she can't accompany us."

"Who are you, miss?" he asked.

"Anna Williams of Lincoln County," Anna replied.

The officer bowed to her, shedding his straw hat. "Captain Miles of the 11th North Carolina. My pleasure." He ran his right hand through his beard.

"And where is your father?"

"With Lee," Anna replied.

"Well, he could be on his way home now," Captain Miles said. "Or maybe he skedaddled to join Joe Johnston, as we plan on doing...It's an awful big country up there..."

Captain Miles took Anna by the arm and led her to a nearby bench where they sat. Settie Two stood nearby, in awe that Anna was talking with an officer.

"We are on our way to join Johnston up near Raleigh. We want to keep the Federals from joining Grant's forces in Virginia."

"But they say the war is over," Anna said.

Captain Miles stiffened. "Not for us."

Anna pressed the captain to be allowed to ride the cars. "I cannot take you. You must return home," Captain Miles said.

Anna was crushed. She was near tears. The cars were her only means of finding her father.

Chapter Four

Anna took Two by the arm and walked outside on the platform to its end, away from the locomotive and cars.

"They will not let us travel on the cars," Anna said. "But we must get to Virginia."

"How we gonna do that?" Two asked. "Your mama sold the mule. We can't walk to Virginia."

"I'm prepared to walk to Virginia, if that's what it takes," Anna said. She noticed that the locomotive had its steam up. "Look, they are getting ready to leave."

The two girls found a perch on an empty wagon nearby and watched as the engine sent billows of steam into the morning sky. The soldiers began shouting to each other to climb on the cars and men were sent running in all directions to round up strays. The girls saw Captain Miles in the midst of the crowd, yelling directions. Anna noticed that there was one main track and a short siding. The engine and cars were on the main track but from the position of the sun overhead she saw that the train was headed southward. That was puzzling. She knew that Raleigh and Virginia were north. There was no way that the engine could change its direction on the one track.

Anna saw the engine shudder into motion—it was pushing the cars backward. It appeared that it would have to move that way until it could find track to turn. That meant that the train would have to go clear to Raleigh before that could happen.

"Two, I have an idea." She explained her plan. The girls sat quietly as the soldiers loaded themselves and their gear on the cars. After a quarter hour it appeared all was ready for the trip. The engineer gave two blasts of his whistle, and the train began backing out of the station, with the cars ahead, filled with the soldiers.

Anna and Two moved right toward the track till they were positioned in front of the locomotive that was slowly moving away .

"When I say, 'Run!'" Anna yelled.

The locomotive was picking up speed, having passed the platform as it headed north out of Charlotte Town.

"Run!" Anna shouted.

The two girls ran down the track between the rails toward the moving engine. They flew down the cross ties about 200 feet and they were at the sloping, black metal fringe that almost touched the rails. This fringe was designed to clear debris from the engine's path. Both girls leaped up its sloping surface, seeking handholds on the hot iron bars. Anna yelped and momentarily let go and began to slip down the iron surface. Two reached out her left arm and grabbed Anna and hauled her up to the narrow platform between the front of the engine's boiler and the fringe. The girls huddled on the platform and braced their feet on the fringe bars. The engine was beginning to rock as it picked up speed. The girls were wide-eyed; they had never moved this fast in their lives. Suddenly, they were surrounded by hot, white steam released from the boiler and spilling over them because of the prevailing wind. They clutched each other and soon the steam blew away.

The houses of Charlotte Town became more scattered as the train moved up the line. Two began to laugh.

"What are you laughing at?" Anna shouted to her.

"We're going backwards," Two said between gulps. "All we can see is where we've been."

Anna laughed. They looked down the track and saw just fields, no people or animals. The two girls clung to the metal bars and laughed as they moved ever backward.

Chapter Five

Settie Two braced herself carefully on the swaying engine. She was almost breathless with excitement. She looked over to Anna and began laughing again, loud choking noises. The thunder of the locomotive covered their laughter. Both girls screamed when the engine pushed the train over wooden bridges that spanned creeks and cuts. They looked down and saw the ground drop off below their feet and saw the flowing water.

Two was glad to be with Anna. By herself she would have been afraid to jump on the engine; by herself she couldn't even think about riding it backwards. She smiled widely at the girl next to her, Anna, with the short hair her mother had cut the week before they left the farm. Two had laughed when she saw Anna's short hair, cut almost as short as a boy's. Anna had been angry that day when Two laughed at her and she chased Two around the yard until she tackled her and sat on her chest.

"Mama says it will be easier to care for this way,"

Anna had said. "You, you don't even have to worry about long hair…" Two knew that was true; her hair was a fuzzy bowl and Settie One cut it with a pair of old shears when it needed cutting, which wasn't often.

Two had been envious of Anna's long hair that was usually braided in a long tail. She was envious when Mrs. Williams washed Anna's hair in the big wood tub under the pin-oak in the yard. Mrs. Williams used homemade soap and it was a long process to get Anna's hair washed and rinsed.

Afterward, the two girls would sit in the sun and talk and laugh as Anna's hair dried.

Two's earliest memories were of Anna. They began just after Mr. Williams brought Settie One and Two to the farm from South Carolina. Two had someone to play with and fight with.

Mr. and Mrs. Williams didn't care that the two girls carried on like sisters. There were no nearby white children for Anna to play with, so Two was a good companion. There were other black children in the neighborhood but Settie One would not let Two leave the farm in daylight and certainly not at night. The two children grew up together. Two slept in the cook house. Anna slept in the big house loft, separated from her parents by a plain plank wall. Each Sunday, they all went to the service at the church by the courthouse. The blacks and whites worshiped in the same church; the blacks went upstairs; the whites downstairs. Two didn't mind being upstairs. She could see the ladies' dresses and the visitors better. In the past years, however, the dresses became shabbier. There were no new ones. Old dresses were patched; everyone had to make do.

Clothing was not a problem for Two. She wore a homespun shirt her mother had made and she had another, a castoff from Anna. She also wore a kind of homespun skirt-pants. She had one pair of homemade shoes for church and Christmas. Other times, Two went barefoot.

The major change in her life came the year before when the Negroes in the neighborhood heard about freedom. The word was passed in the night, among friends. The Negroes knew that to talk of freedom in daylight was to invite a beating or worse. Freedom was a condition none of them knew. They had heard of free men, usually granted by masters to older slaves, and of craftsmen in the cities, like Charleston, that allowed them to come and go as they pleased. The condition of slavery in their experience, however, was from birth to the grave. They were owned by another and it was a permanent knot around their necks. Two occasionally asked Mrs. Williams about the Yankees and their peculiar ideas, hoping that she would explain how the Yankees, who lived far away, could make slaves free. And, more important, what it all meant? The idea of freedom was strange to Two. Did it mean she would have to leave the farm? It was all the life she knew. Would she have to leave her mother? What would she do? She was not trained for anything. She would have to find work in the fields. But where? Two decided that freedom was for big people. She would worry about it when she got big. Until then, she would enjoy her days with Anna.

Two felt thrilled to be on such an adventure with Anna. They were like sisters, though white and black. With Anna, Two didn't feel like a slave. The girls dressed alike. Anna wore homespun, too—blouse and cotton skirt made from an old dress of Mrs. Williams'. Anna wore shoes, ankle-high that had been cobbled for her by an itinerant peddler the year before. Two was envious of Anna's shoes. They had leather laces and were dark brown, though scuffed now.

The rocking motion of the engine was lulling. Two felt herself getting drowsy in the strong sunlight. She estimated it was getting toward noon. Settie One had taught Two how to tell "field time," the way Negroes told time when they were working the crops. Negro time began before daybreak, when field hands would rise, dress and prepare for their day of planting, clearing, hoeing, or picking cotton. When the sun was high in the sky, it was time for the noon dinner, which was usually cooked food packed in a cloth and set in the nearest shade. Or, sometimes, at harvest, the meal was carried to the hands by wagon and ladled out to them where they stood. Negroes worked until just before sunset, if the weather was good. They walked to their cabins where they had their evening meal. In good weather, the field hands sat outside their cabins by small fires and told stories.

Only the most venturesome field hands tried to

travel to other farms after the day; they could be stopped on the road by patrollers and taken in chains. Two often had nightmares about the "pattyrollers." Anna sometimes laughed at the way Two pronounced words. Both girls spoke with languid, slurring drawls but Two had a way of mangling words.

"Girl," Settie One would say, "You must be churning butter in your mouth." Yet they all could understand what Two meant.

Two raised her head and tried to shade her eyes to get a fix on the sun. It was definitely overhead. Two had no idea how long they had been riding the engine or how far it was to Raleigh. She had no idea where Raleigh was, or Virginia, for that matter. Didn't matter. She was with Anna.

The girls felt a change in the rumble and rock of the engine beneath their bottoms. The brush beside the tracks began to move past slower. The locomotive was slowing. Two saw that Anna was peering around the engine's boiler, to see what was happening. Two was afraid Anna would be seen and their perch discovered. She was afraid of what might happen then.

The engine slowed gradually, chuffing and puffing, with steam again billowing over the girls because of the wind. Soon the girls saw houses by the track side and in the distance, a road. The engine jerked to a stop, moved and stopped again. Two peered around her side of the boiler and saw that the rear of the engine was stopped near a large wood tub that stood on poles above the boiler. It was a frightening sight and Two didn't know what it was. She motioned to Anna, who clambered across Two to look.

"It's a water tank," Anna said. "Papa told me they have them to put water in the boiler to make steam." Two was reassured by Anna's explanation. The girls saw the engineer hop down from his cab ahead and pull a rope that was attached to a long tin pipe from the tub. He guided the pipe to the top of the engine.

Anna peered around the other side of the engine and saw that the train was stopped near a small wood shed and road that crossed the tracks. There was a sign painted on the shed and by squinting she made out the name, "Salisbury." Behind the shed the hilly ground rose through the blooming trees, with the road following the rise. Ahead, she saw more buildings, including one large dark building that seemed threatening. Anna could see figures walking along the road, headed to the train. As they got closer, Anna saw that many were limping, many walking without shoes, many holding each other for support. Many were in tatters; but Anna saw with shock that the closest men were coming toward the train in blue uniforms. Yankees!

Chapter Six

Anna peered around the engine boiler as the mob of tattered Yankees swarmed to the train. She counted more than 20 men, most looking like ill-clothed scarecrows from the fields. Then, with a clatter, Captain Miles and a few of his men climbed down from the cars ahead.

"Halt!" the captain yelled.

Some of the Yankees slowed; others kept stumbling toward the cars until the leading men surrounded the Confederate officer.

One Yankee, a large, bearded man with three upraised stripes on his coat, yelled to Miles.

"We're freed prisoners of war, from the stockade here in Salisbury. They let us go and told us we could take the cars to Virginia or to find Sherman's army…"

Captain Miles straightened himself and drew his sword. "I don't care who you are; I am in command of this train and no Yankees will ride on it today…"

"But the war is over," the large Yankee bellowed at Miles.

"Not for us, it isn't," Captain Miles said. "Maybe for General Lee in Virginia but we're joining General Johnston."

Some of the Yankee soldiers tried to climb into the cars.

"My men will shoot if you don't climb down," Miles yelled. With that, muskets were pushed out some of the windows, causing the released prisoners to back up with some stumbling on the track side.

Anna turned to Two and put her finger to her lips for silence. Anna was afraid that some of the Yankees would move toward their perch and discover them. When she peered around the boiler she saw Captain Miles moving toward the locomotive. The engineer leaned out of his station and when Miles was close enough, he yelled, "Get this train moving…" The engineer nodded. Suddenly, the whistle blew two short blasts and the girls felt the locomotive begin to shudder as the wheels began to turn.

"Get down," Anna shouted to Two. The girls huddled together, trying to make themselves as small as possible on their perch. They realized that when the train passed the mob of Yankees they would be seen on the front of the engine.

They were seen but the mass of men seemed too dazed to do or say anything as the engine rolled by them. The locomotive picked up speed. The engine was nearly past the freed prisoners when the tall man with the stripes ran onto the track and as the girls had done, ran toward the locomotive. Anna saw that his long strides would carry him to the engine if his energy didn't fail.

The tall man reached the sloping iron grid just in time and began pulling himself upward toward the girls' perch. The other prisoners, stunned by Captain Miles' refusal to carry them and by the train's departure, came to life too late. By the time the group realized they could do what the tall soldier had done, the train had left the small depot and was moving too fast. Some ran anyway, a few staggering and falling from the exertion. Soon the engine was rocking across a wood trestle bridge across a deep cut and the prisoners were left in the distance.

The tall Yankee carefully moved up to the narrow platform and, turning, placed his boots firmly in the iron grid for support. He stared at the girls silently. They stared back as the train swayed along the track.

Anna saw their companion was filthy, his uniform coat was ripped in places and he had dark smudges on his hollow cheeks. His beard was ragged, uncut and he was hatless. The coat was dark blue, his trousers a lighter blue but equally dirty. The man stared at the girls with intensity, his eyes marked by dark rings. To Anna he seemed all beard and eyes and little else. The girls had heard much of the Yankees over the years; that they were damnable creations, sent to force free men into a union they didn't want. Yankees were the enemy; they were devils and since 1864, the worst Yankees were the forces of General Sherman, the devil's own, who burned and ruined Atlanta and Columbia, South Carolina. Sherman's army, Anna heard, had ripped a path 100 miles wide in Georgia to the sea and up into the Carolinas. This soldier before her seemed the very embodiment of the evil she had heard about. And now he was within arm's length of her. Anna thought of kicking out suddenly, hoping to dislodge their unwelcome companion, causing him to tumble from the engine onto the track side or a ravine. Anna decided against it; she didn't think she had the strength and she didn't know what he would do if she moved. He might have a knife or a gun.

The soldier raised his right hand and slipped it into his jacket. Anna caught her breath. The hand slowly reappeared, holding a large piece of bread. The soldier looked at it and began to eat hungrily. He made noises in his throat like an animal, Anna noticed. Soon the bread was gone.

"Hungry," he said, looking back at the girls.

He made a brief smile before his wild beard covered his mouth.

"Where is this train going?" the soldier asked in a strange, flat accent that the girls had never heard before. Yankees, Anna decided, even sound different.

"Raleigh," Anna said loudly over the engine noise.

The soldier nodded. "Why are you riding out here?" he asked.

The girls did not reply. The train rocked on for more miles. Anna began to feel drowsy in the bright

45

sun. She fought to stay awake; she knew if she napped she would lose her hold and slip from the engine.

Anna kept awake by counting the houses and barns the train passed. Not many, she saw as the train chugged northward.

"What's the next stop?" the Yankee asked.

"I don't know," Anna replied. "They said the train would go to Raleigh…"

"I doubt if we'll get that far, if General Sherman is in the neighborhood," the soldier said.

"You have nothing to worry about if you're with me," he added with another smile. "What's your name?"

Anna told him her name and pointed to Two and gave her name. The soldier looked puzzled.

"Two," Anna said. "Her mother is One.

The soldier laughed. Two flashed angry eyes at him.

They felt the train change its rocking motion—it was slowing. A mile or so down the track it stopped. The Yankee peered around the engine.

"Oh, oh," he said.

Anna heard voices. "Need more wood," the engineer said to someone. "Have your men chop some trees."

Anna looked to the track side growth, wondering if she and Two could hide there until the soldiers chopped their wood and got the train moving.

Before she could decide she heard the crunching of gravel and the figure of Captain Miles appeared around the boiler.

"What have we here?" he boomed, more startled by the two girls and shabby Yankee than they were of him.

"You, there, get down," Miles waved at the Yankee. Miles reached for his holster.

"No need for that, colonel, I'm unarmed, and a released prisoner. I've had my share of fighting..." the Yankee said.

Miles turned back to the cars and yelled, "Sergeant!" He took off his hat and wiped the inside band before speaking again, this time to Anna.

"You mean you've been riding on this engine since we left Charlotte Town?"

Anna nodded yes.

"You could have been killed," the captain said as the his sergeant marched up to the officer. The tall sergeant seemed as surprised as Miles to see the trio.

"Well, get down, all of you," he commanded. Miles turned to the sergeant. "Get the men to chopping wood for the boiler or we'll not get to Joe Johnston today." The sergeant nodded rapidly and walked back to the cars. Soon Anna heard his bark as he pushed men from the train.

Anna, Two and the Yankee stood with Captain Miles.

"I must get to Virginia," Anna said to Miles.

He looked down at her with a serious face. "There is no possibility you can come with us. We are joining Joe Johnston and that means battle."

"But, the war is over," the Yankee said.

Captain Miles returned his pistol to its holster.

"General Lee surrendered, not Joe Johnston." Miles stamped his feet nervously. Anna could see he was angry.

"Dammit. As you are a released prisoner, I am at a hard place here. I don't want to take you prisoner again. I have no room for prisoners. Have you been paroled?"

The Yankee nodded no. "Released, without restrictions," he said softly. Captain Miles walked away, obviously agitated and then he returned to face the trio.

"The road to Greensboro is over yonder. Get started on it and don't look back, all three of you…"

Anna was about to protest when she saw from Captain Miles' face it would do no good.

The two girls hitched their cotton bags to a more comfortable position on their sides and with the tall Yankee in the lead, headed for the road through the brush. They could hear the soldiers chopping wood and their muffled curses.

They found the road about a quarter of a mile to the west, a narrow, rutted path no wider than a country wagon and nothing in sight.

They trudged for some miles, passing only one abandoned farm house. There was no one abroad on the highway. The sky darkened; they saw heavy, dark clouds moving from the west bringing the threat of a spring storm. Anna and Two knew how quickly these could form in the country. One minute bright sunlight and the next, heavy downpour and a strong wind.

"Best we find shelter," Anna said.

The Yankee grunted.

"Gonna rain for sure," Two said.

A half mile farther down the road they saw a house on a nearby hill. There was a path leading to it and they climbed the path. There was a mule in a corral by the side of the barn. There was a main house, large but unpainted, the barn and corral and a few outbuildings in the rear. The three stepped up on the wide, covered porch.

"Hello!" the Yankee called. They heard something move inside the house. Anna went to a large side window and peered in. She saw a bare room with a few chairs. "Hello!" the Yankee called again.

Suddenly, the front door flew open and the muzzle of a musket sprang out of the interior darkness at them.

"Don't shoot," the Yankee said, throwing his hands in the air. "We mean no harm. There are children here with me…"

"What do you mean, children?" the unseen speaker said. "You're a Sherman 'bummer,' here to rob me of my last possessions. I've heard about you 'bummers.'"

"I'm no 'bummer,'" the Yankee said. "I've just been released from the Salisbury Prison and with these two children, we've been thrown off the Raleigh train. I'm trying to get home…"

"Where's home?" the voice asked.

"Rhode Island," the soldier said. "My people are from Coventry. And I'm sorry I didn't join the Navy, instead of the Second Rhode Island."

Anna hoped his soothing but strange voice would cause the musket holder to put the weapon down.

Anna had never had the muzzle of a weapon aimed at her. It was frightening.

"How many are with you?" the voice asked. Anna suspected it was a woman, despite the deep growl.

"Just what you see," the Yankee said. "The musket is frightening the children…"

The figure stepped closer to the doorway and light. Anna saw it was a woman, tall and bent, with gray hair wrapped in a bun atop her head and wearing a long, gray dress that had seen better days. The musket remained aimed at the three.

"Don't want no Yankees," the woman said.

"We stopped because of the storm," the soldier said, seconds before the first flash of lightning split the afternoon sky. "We need directions to Raleigh," he added.

"Raleigh," the old woman spat. "You're no closer to Raleigh than to heaven."

"Can you spare us some food, drink?" the soldier asked. "For the children," he added.

"Not for no Yankee children," the woman spat.

Anna bristled. "Ain't no Yankee," she replied loudly. "My father is with General Lee. We're going to meet him…"

The woman looked at her. "That so?" she said. "You don't sound like a Yankee, that's for sure. And this gal…?"

"She's with me," Anna said. "Her mother is my mother's servant. We are traveling together."

"Well, ain't that a pleasure," the woman said. "We don't have no Negroes. They all run off when they heard Sherman was acomin'. Left me here to run this place alone." The musket wavered in her hands. Finally, she upended it and put it against the wall. "Ain't loaded. Come in, maybe you can help me."

The three entered the house past the woman in the doorway as the first large, heavy raindrops began to splatter on the front porch.

They stood nervously in the hallway, uncertain which way to go.

"Negro gal can go in the kitchen, back there," the woman said, pointing down the hall. Two looked at Anna, who nodded yes. "Yawl," the woman said to Anna and the Yankee, "can sit a spell in the parlor;" she indicated with her right arm, a room to the right of the hall. It was furnished with three pieces of furniture, a high sofa of a hairy, brushy material, pale green, and two matching chairs of a dark red material. The furniture, Anna saw, had large carved claw feet. "Sit you down," the woman ordered, taking one of the chairs.

Anna and the Yankee gingerly sat on the sofa. Anna felt and heard her stomach growl. It had been many hours since breakfast. She was hungry.

"My sons off to the war, too," the woman said softly.

"The war is over," the Yankee said.

"We have no such word," the woman said.

"Yes," he added. "The news came by telegraph to Salisbury. That's why we got released. General Lee signed with General Grant up in Virginia. It's over. Thank God."

"My boys be comin' back to me?" the woman said. The Yankee looked at Anna and nodded yes.

"Thank the Lord," the woman said. Anna thought she would cry. Her hands, kept in her lap, now began to move in the air.

"They took my 16-year-old. His brother went two years ago. Last I heard he was at Petersburg, with his father. He could write. Did last month, or was it two months. My husband, he can't write…I don't know where my 16-year-old is. They said they would take him for the state militia, that he would most likely be guarding Greensboro with Wheeler and them…"

"Wheeler?" the Yankee asked.

"General Joe Wheeler," the woman said. "His horsemen came up a few weeks ago and said they needed every man for defense. That Sherman was coming up from Columbia and he would tear up the country with his bummers. That they was killing women and children and stealin' everything. Showed me a newspaper from Charlotte Town that warned all the people about it." She stopped and said a moment later. "Read it to me. I can't read." She abruptly rose and walked to the hall.

"But they left it here. You can see." She disappeared into the hall. Anna looked at the Yankee, who shrugged. The woman returned holding a small two-sided, one-page newspaper. She handed it to the Yankee, who looked it over without word for a few minutes.

"Yes," he said at length, "it does report that General

Sherman has taken Columbia and that he burned the city. It warns all Carolinians to beware Sherman's 'bummers,' as they are raiding through the country. Charlotte Town is in the way of his forces…" The Yankee dropped the newspaper. "But it's dated in March and I don't think Sherman got to Charlotte. He didn't get to Salisbury, I'm sure."

The woman nodded to the Yankee. "Thank you for reading that to me. I had to get a neighbor lady read my son's letters. I was embarrassed. Grew up in this county; didn't go to school because there wasn't a school."

"That's all right, ma'am," the Yankee said. He cleared his throat. "Could we trouble you for something to eat. I'm sure the children are hungry…."

Anna disliked being called a child but she didn't protest. She was too hungry.

The woman waved her hands nervously. "Well, I've got some side and 'taters. Cooked the 'taters this morning. You're welcome to have some." She stood and waved the man and girl to follow her to the kitchen.

They found Two seated on a stool, staring out the back window at the rain. Two jumped off the stool when she heard the woman enter the kitchen.

"I'll fry up some 'side and there's a bit of bread in the pantry. I still have some churn butter in the spring house, if the gal will go fetch it."

Anna and Two helped the woman prepare the meal. Two set the table in the kitchen, using the woman's meager crockery and utensils.

They sat at the table as the woman spooned out the

cooked bacon and gravy over the potatoes.

Anna was famished and she could see Two was as hungry. When the woman sat, the soldier bowed his head and said, "Thank you, Lord for this lady's charity toward us and help us to be as kind." It was a short prayer and Anna was impressed. She didn't think Yankees prayed.

"Thank you," the woman said with the first smile they had seen since they arrived. The three began to eat. Two had her plate on the floor against the wall. The rain drummed on the roof.

Anna cut the thick bacon and savored it, chewing slowly and absorbing all the taste. The potatoes were lumpy but tasty with the bacon gravy on them.

"There's more, young'un," the woman said to her when she cleaned her plate. Then the woman turned to the Yankee.

"I don't think we gave our names. I'm Mary Crimes. My husband is John Crimes, though they call him Jack…"

The Yankee stood, embarrassed. "Yes, ma'am. I'm Sergeant William Caldwell, though they call me Bill. And this…" he began but Anna interrupted him and stood. Anna gave her name and home and introduced Two. "She's called Two because her mother is One." It sounded humorous and Sergeant Caldwell smiled.

"Why are you young'uns out tramping the country? Mrs. Crimes asked.

Anna explained that they had set off to find her father when her mother took sick in Charlotte Town.

"Oh, child," Mrs. Crimes said. "It's a big country up there in Virginia. How are you going to find your father?" Anna had no reply.

The sound of rain on the roof was loud in their ears. "Well, y'all can't go abroad in this weather," Mrs. Crimes said. "I'll fix my son's bed for the girl. The Negro gal can sleep on the floor here in the kitchen. "You," she said, turning to Sergeant Caldwell, "can sleep in the parlor on the sofa. I'll fix a quilt for you."

"Thank you, ma'am," he said. Mrs. Crimes turned to Two on the floor. "Gal, you collect the plates and take them out to the spring house and wash 'em good."

Darkness came with the storm and by the time Mrs. Crimes had the visitors installed in the various beds it was blackness outside. Mrs. Crimes used a small candle nub to show Anna the small upstairs room with the sloping roof. It contained a bed, chair and a small, rough-hewn table. "My son used to write his letters on that table when he was a tad," Mrs. Crimes said.

Anna shed her blouse and skirt and crawled into the bed. Its straw mattress reminded her of her own and in a moment she was struck with emotion and longing for home and her parents. She fought back a sob and the tears sure to follow.

Crying, she thought, would not find her father quicker. She said a quick prayer that she would find him soon and they would return safely home. "And keep mother well," she added.

Chapter Seven

They were on the Greensboro Road shortly after sunrise the next morning, refreshed by the sleep. Mrs. Crimes had fried some eggs that made a good breakfast before marching on the road. The rain had ended in the night and the morning air was sweet and clean. Mrs. Crimes gave Sergeant Caldwell directions to Greensboro. The route was due north.

After an hour on the road they heard a wagon behind them and turned to see it pulled by an old mule and directed by an old man.

Sergeant Caldwell called him to a stop. "Can you give us a ride to Greensboro?" he asked, waving to the girls.

The old man looked at Caldwell and asked, "Soldier?"

"Was," Caldwell replied. "It's over now. I'm going home…" The old man waved them into the back of the wagon. There were four burlap bags in the wagon. "'Taters I'm taking up to Greensboro Town to sell for cash. Ain't seen no cash for almost a year," the old fellow said. The girls made themselves comfortable and Caldwell lay down on the bed of the wagon and was asleep quickly. Anna studied his face. It had a yellow pallor and was thin. The Yankee snored through his long nose. Sergeant Caldwell was a Yankee but he was pleasant enough company on their journey, Anna thought. Especially if the war was over and there was no more reason to hate Yankees.

Anna didn't think she hated Yankees. In truth, she had never met a Yankee before Sergeant Caldwell. They were spoken of as devils, with horns and tails, doing the Devil's work. But the sergeant seemed normal to her. Yankees freed the slaves, Anna knew, and that caused many slaves to run away. Anna's family was lucky that Settie One and Two had not run away. Maybe they didn't know where to go, she thought.

"Do you know you're free now?" she asked Two. The black girl smiled and nodded yes.

"Do you want to run away?" Anna asked. Two's eyes widened.

"No, Anna. I want to go with you on your adventure. And then I want to go back on the farm with Settie and live there."

"But you could go north and find a new home and maybe new people..." Anna persisted. Two shook her head vigorously.

"What would I do there?" she replied.

"You could go to school, maybe get paid for being a servant," Anna said.

"We not allowed to read or write," Two said.

"Now you can. The old days are over," Anna said.

"Seems like the same days to me," Two answered.

They fell silent. Anna wondered if she would be able to get back on the train in Greensboro. She wondered how far Greensboro was from Raleigh and both from Virginia. The world, she decided, was a big place and there seemed no end to it. The wagon's rocking and the sun high in the sky lulled the girls to sleep and the hours passed. Anna awakened with the bark of the old man, "Comin' to town," he said.

Anna saw the rutted, muddy wide street and cluster of unpainted houses, just like Charlotte Town. The tallest building was a whitewashed church with a tall spire. The houses had pastures behind them, with cattle and outbuildings and barns. It was Greensboro but Anna decided it wasn't much. The old driver let them off by a hotel and mercantile store. Sergeant Caldwell climbed down stiffly and helped the girls.

"Thanks, old man," Caldwell said to the driver, who waved and flicked his long stick at the mule.

The trio stood in the mud and looked around at the town. There wasn't much to see. Two horses were tied to the hitch in front of the mercantile. "Let's try the hotel," Caldwell said, walking up the wood steps and cleaning his boots on the metal ridge before the door. They stepped into a large open room with scattered chairs on the bare wood floor. A bearded man stood at the back of the room, behind a board table.

"Yes?" he asked in a high, thin voice.

"We'd like some information," Sergeant Caldwell asked.

"Are you from Sherman's Army?" the hotel clerk asked in a louder voice.

"No," Caldwell replied. "We're passing through…"

The clerk came toward them brandishing a long-barrel Colt pistol in his right hand.

"We're expecting Sherman any moment now. Y'awl look like Yankees to me," he said.

"Well, I'm a Yankee," Caldwell said. "Unarmed. Released prisoner of war. The war is over. Haven't you people heard that yet?"

"The telegraph has been cut for some days now," the clerk said. "Joe Wheeler's soldiers came through and said that Joe Johnston was still fighting Sherman."

"Where is Sherman?" Caldwell asked.

"Don't know," the clerk said. "Don't care to find out. People been coming here, saying that they have been burned out, robbed and in some cases murdered… Sherman is the very devil."

"Well, we ain't out for that mischief. We want to get to Raleigh and I want to get back to Rhode Island," Caldwell said.

"Well, you're not going anywhere right now," the clerk said, aiming the pistol at Caldwell's stomach. At the same moment the door opened and three men entered carrying muskets.

"Yankee bummer, Bob?"

"Guess so," the clerk answered. "Says he's bound for Rhode Island."

"He's bound for hell, is where he's bound," a large, fat man dressed in a tight black suit said, prodding Caldwell with his weapon.

"Take him out back and hang him," the fat man said to the others. "Maybe if we leave enough bummers in the trees the others will stop their pillaging."

Anna was shocked. They couldn't just hang the sergeant. He had not done anything to warrant hanging. She was about to speak when the two men prodded Caldwell toward the back of the building. Two stared at the scene with wide eyes.

"Excuse me," Caldwell said, stopping. "Before you hang me, could I say good-bye to my daughter?"

"Your daughter?" the fat man asked.

"Yes," Caldwell said, turning toward Anna. "This girl came all the way to Salisbury, to the prison, to see me released. You men can't be heartless enough to hang a man before he has a chance to say good-bye to his child…."

The fat man stared at Caldwell and turned to Anna.

"You came to Salisbury, to the prison…?" he asked.

Anna nodded yes. It wasn't a lie; he hadn't asked if she was Caldwell's daughter. The fat man seemed unsure of what to do next. Anna moved closer to Caldwell. He bent down and whispered. "I'm going to make a run for it. You and Two run the other way. I don't want you getting in the way of any bullets…"

Anna nodded. The fat man waved his pistol and Caldwell and the girls moved toward the hotel's front door. As they stepped out on the porch they heard yelling up the street.

"Yankees coming!" someone was screaming at the top of their voice. The screamer, a thin fellow dressed in vagabond clothing ran past them as they heard the clatter of horses turn onto the street 200 yards away. The horsemen were dressed in blue, dark shirts and light blue trousers and they came at a gallop.

"Yankees," the fat man gasped before he ran from the porch and around the building. The other men followed him.

The horsemen were four abreast and they rode past Caldwell and the two girls on the porch. A single horseman approached. He wore a small peaked cap and a sword. In his hand he held a Colt revolver similar to the fat man's.

Anna saw that he wore a short coat, had a dark beard and was a big, angry fellow.

"Any rebel cavalry here?" the man asked Caldwell.

"No. But the fellows around back were about to hang me…," Caldwell said with a smile.

"Damn them," the big man yelled, as he swiveled in his saddle to yell at the passing troop, "Sergeant, 'round back, bring me those men…"

Anna watched as the sergeant yelled more commands and horsemen moved at the gallop around the side of the building.

"Kirkpatrick," the big man said. "Colonel Kirkpatrick and this is the Second Cavalry. We're out for Wheeler's people."

Caldwell took a step forward. "Sergeant Caldwell, released prisoner of war from Salisbury Prison. I was headed home," he said, waving his left arm at Anna and Two, "when I met up with these two young rebel ladies on the train. We got here and some men tried to hang me..."

"We'll see about that!" the colonel said. At that moment the troopers returned, prodding the fat man and the thin man with their short rifles.

"Inside," Kirkpatrick said to his sergeant, as he dismounted. Anna was amazed by the size of the man. He towered over Caldwell, whom he took by the arm. Once inside, Kirkpatrick turned to his sergeant and said, "Send a detail through this God-forsaken place and see if you can flush any of Wheeler's people."

Then Kirkpatrick turned to the fat man and asked, "Well, what do you have to say for yourself?" Anna saw that the fat man was flushed from running and winded. He didn't respond.

"Civilians who hang unarmed prisoners are flying the black flag, and will be treated as such. Do you know what that means?" Kirkpatrick yelled in a voice that made Anna and Two startle.

"We thought..." the fat man stuttered.

"What?" Kirkpatrick yelled.

"We thought he was one of Sherman's bummers...."

Kirkpatrick looked at the fat man a moment and said in a soft voice, "I'm one of General Sherman's bummers, you damned Confederate lout. You ignorant fool. You damned Confederates don't even know the war is over and Lee surrendered." Kirkpatrick paused, then asked, "What do you do here?"

Anna saw the fat man's sweat roll down his face. "I'm bailiff at the court…"

"Well, Mr. Bailiff," Kirkpatrick said, "the war is over and you are at the mercy of General Sherman's military government. I ought to hang you but as you didn't hang Sergeant Caldwell here, I think I'll have my troops take you over to your courthouse and lock you up. Sergeant!" he yelled, loud enough for the men outside to hear. The bulky sergeant came stomping into the hotel lobby.

"Take this riffraff and lock 'em up. Search 'em first for more weapons and anything else that might help us find Wheeler."

The thin man took this time to speak up. "But you can't arrest me. I run this hotel and…."

"Shut up!" the Federal officer boomed in his face. "You don't run anything. This is my hotel from this minute on. And," he said, waving his right arm, "if I decide to, I might just burn this place down, furniture and all." Anna saw that the thin man appeared faint.

The bulky sergeant prodded the fat man with his short rifle and the two were hustled out of the building.

"Damn fools they are," Kirkpatrick said, looking at Anna closely, his angry face softening in a smile. "And what kind of Bonnie Rebel Girl do we have here?"

Anna politely introduced herself and Two. Kirkpatrick motioned them all to nearby plush chairs. "Take a seat till we get this all thrashed out." They sat as commanded.

Before another word was spoken, another sergeant came crashing into the lobby. "Colonel, some women out here want to know if you plan to burn the town and steal their valuables."

"Dammit-to-hell," Kirkpatrick flushed red and half-rising from his chair, yelled, "Tell them we are not going to burn their town and steal their valuables. Tell them the damn war is over as soon as we get all of Wheeler's people to lay down their arms." The colonel then turned to Caldwell. "Tell me your story." He listened as Caldwell explained their journey thus far.

"Well, you can ride with us today. Don't think we can leave you here; those bushwhackers will grab you sure, Bonnie Rebels or not," he added, smiling at Anna. She tried to smile back at the big man but he was so intimidating that Anna was frightened. Up close she saw his dark eyes, black beard, tanned skin, large nose, big white teeth, and she was afraid. Kirkpatrick looked like the killers Yankees were reputed to be.

The big man shook his head. "This war is over and I think the peace here is going to be as troublesome as the war was. These people don't understand any-thing…" With that Kirkpatrick yelled outside for food and soon they were eating bread, cheese and some cooked eggs. Anna and Two ate quickly, realizing how hungry they were. Kirkpatrick called for horses and soon the two girls were sharing a military saddle on a tall cavalry horse. Caldwell rode another Yankee mount, tall and healthy, Anna noticed. Their animals were healthy and a contrast to the thin horses and mules she had seen thus far in her travel.

Kirkpatrick wheeled his mount and stopped by them. "We will circle the country this afternoon and return to our base. You should find it interesting," he winked at the girls. "I have the most beautiful young lady in the Confederacy there."

Anna and Caldwell looked at each other in puzzlement.

Chapter Eight

Riding with the cavalry was exhilarating for Anna and Two. They found themselves in the rear of the formation and every once in a while a trooper would hoot and yell at them. At first the girls were frightened until they saw that the men meant no harm. They were in good spirits. As the sun began its slide down in the west, Anna noted that the troop had swung around to the east and began moving at a faster gallup. The horses seemed to sense they were close to their corrals and feeding.

The troop was moving four abreast down a narrow country road when Anna saw Col. Kirkpatrick wheel his horse to the right into a lane that bordered a large field that held wagons and soldiers. At the end of the lane was a large brick house, the largest Anna had ever seen. It took her breath away. At the end of the lane was a circular gravel driveway that led to the front door.

The troopers stopped and lowered the split rail fencing and moved into the field. Anna saw farriers and their forges for shoeing the animals. She smelled cooking, from large black pots under tents hoisted on tall poles. The troopers dismounted and began caring for their animals, stripping them of saddles and weapons at their sergeants' calls.

Col. Kirkpatrick galloped to where Anna and Two watched the military display. Sergeant Caldwell rode beside him.

"You will stay with me in the house," Kirkpatrick said. He waved them to follow him up the lane. As she got closer, Anna was more impressed by the house. Its window sills were painted and she counted 16 windows in two rows. The house had two large chimneys, one at each end. Anna had never seen such a house. The girls dismounted and handed their reins to a soldier who smiled down at them and walked their horse to the corral in the field.

Once inside, Anna saw that the smooth wood floors were dirty from the soldiers' boots.

"This place belongs to a fellow in the governor's cabinet. He's up at Raleigh now, so we took it over. It's not the Astor Hotel but it'll do," Kirkpatrick said. "Daniels," he bellowed.

A figure appeared in the doorway, a tall soldier the size of Kirkpatrick. "Show these girls where they can wash up and bring my whiskey and two glasses." The soldier nodded and waved to Anna. The girls followed the big man out of the room and down a long, wide corridor to the back of the house. He took them down outside steps to the spring house, where he lowered a wood bucket and pulled up water for a white basin.

Once it was nearly full he pointed toward it. "Soap there, too," the soldier said in a deep voice. Anna had never seen soap so white it looked like cream. She picked it up and felt its slipperiness. There were white cotton towels next to the basin. The girls took turns washing their faces and hands. They were dirty from the ride. Washed and dried they felt refreshed. They walked back inside the house. Anna could see that Two was nervous about being in the building. "It's all right," Anna reassured her.

They found Kirkpatrick and Caldwell where they had left them. The colonel stood and bowed. He had removed his sword and it lay on the floor by his chair. "The Bonnie Rebel has returned." He motioned her to a chair. Two retreated to the nearest wall and slid down it to sit on the floor.

"Now, tell us your story again with all the details," the colonel said. Anna recounted the trip from the farm to Charlotte and the events of the last day.

"We don't have troops in Charlotte yet. That town escaped the perils of war, unlike Atlanta and Raleigh," Kirkpatrick said.

"General Lee has surrendered his troops. They have been paroled to return to their homes with as many animals as they have, which are precious few." The colonel slammed his big fist on the chair arm. "This is a damnable confusing time. The war is over," he said, jabbing his finger at Caldwell. "But Joe Johnston and Joe Wheeler want to continue the fight. Johnston met with General Sherman outside Raleigh and agreed to the same terms General Grant gave Lee.

"However, those damn fools in Washington refuse to honor it. The Secretary of War says General Sherman didn't have authority to sue for peace with Johnston. So, technically, we are still at war. And," Kirkpatrick growled, "much of Lee's army will be passing through our lines on their way home. How can we tell friend from foe?" Kirkpatrick was silent a moment. "It seems all very strange since Mr. Lincoln was assassinated..."

Caldwell leaned forward with a start. "Assassinated?"

"Yes," the colonel said. "At some theater in Washington. Last Friday. Our forces are looking for an actor named John Booth. Saw him in New York once. He shot the President."

Anna looked at Two, wondering what was happening. It was all rushing together—Lee surrendering, Lincoln shot to death, the war over but it was not.

"Sergeant," Kirkpatrick continued, "I'll get you over to Raleigh and on a train to Wilmington, if the army has it running again. From there you can get a steamer and maybe get to New York or even Providence."

Caldwell cupped his hands, as if in prayer. "If I could get to Providence by steamer I would consider it a gift from the Lord. After a year at Salisbury I'm afraid my family believes me dead. So many of our regiment did die."

The colonel rubbed his face. "No sense in keeping you with us. We're regulars but the other armies and regiments will be folding their tents quickly, the better to get home." As he finished his thought, Anna saw Kirkpatrick's face explode in a grimace that passed for a smile. Anna turned and saw the most beautiful woman she had ever seen in her life, standing in the doorway, dressed in a pale lavender dress.

The woman had golden hair that was done up in braids atop her head. Her most attractive and startling feature were bright blue eyes set amid creamy skin. Her presence stopped conversation as the two men and two girls stared at the sight. Caldwell jumped to his feet with embarrassment. The colonel stood and bowed.

"May I present Miss Frances Hitchcock of Charleston and Columbia and soon-to-be, of Philadelphia." Caldwell bowed to the vision. Kirkpatrick introduced Caldwell and the girls. Frances Hitchcock walked to Anna and took her hand. "So pleased to meet you, my dear," she said in a soft drawl. Frances nodded to Caldwell, still standing. The colonel placed Frances in a chair. The young woman arranged herself with such majesty and elegance that Anna was unable to keep her eyes from her.

"They are our guests for dinner," Kirkpatrick said. The colonel and Caldwell finished their whiskeys before the colonel's man, Daniels, entered the room to say that dinner was ready. Daniels motioned to Two to follow him. Anna went with the adults to an adjoining room that startled Anna. It contained dark, graceful chairs and the largest table she had ever seen. A tall side table contained glasses and plates. As dusk fell the room was brightened by candles in silver holders. The supper consisted of beef stew and fresh bread. It was plain but Anna had not had such delicious food in many months. She watched as Kirkpatrick passed the wine bottle to Caldwell, after pouring a glass for Miss Hitchcock.

"Enlisted men mess separately, but I guess that after that prison and almost being hanged today, you deserve a good meal," the colonel said before asking Caldwell about conditions in the prison. Miss Hitchcock was silent through the meal.

When they had finished eating Kirkpatrick looked up and said to the young woman, "Please arrange for this young Rebel to bed down somewhere upstairs. I don't want her out in the fields with the men." Anna noticed a mild irritation pass over Miss Hitchcock's face quickly before she smiled at Anna.

"Please come with me," she said, rising from her chair.

They climbed the stairs. "Can Two stay with me?" she asked the woman.

"Who?" Miss Hitchcock asked without turning.

"My servant," Anna said.

"Servants sleep out back," the woman said as they reached the darkened upstairs hallway. Miss Hitchcock opened a door and found an oil lamp that she lit with a large wood match that Anna recognized as a "Lucifer." The lamp cast an orange glow in the room, which Anna saw contained two plush chairs, a settee, a large bed and two trunks.

"Do you really live here?" Anna asked.

Miss Hitchcock laughed. "No. I lived in Charleston until Sherman came and then we went to Columbia. I'm traveling with the colonel to Philadelphia. He took my mother and me out of Columbia while it was burning. My mother is from Philadelphia. My father was from Charleston and we lived there through this awful war. We wanted to go north but it was impossible. Now, it's possible."

"Where is your mother now?" Anna asked.

"She took our carriage and went to Raleigh to see about passage to Philadelphia." Anna nodded, wondering why Miss Hitchcock hadn't gone with her? And wondering why someone from Charleston wanted to go to Philadelphia? But she didn't ask. It seemed strange to Anna that this Charleston lady would be traveling with the Yankee army. But everything that had happened this day was strange.

Anna followed Miss Hitchcock out of her room and down the corridor to a smaller room at the end of the hall. "This, I believe, is the children's room," she said, pointing out the small corner bed.

Anna nodded and turned to the door. "Where are you going?" the woman asked.

"I have to go out back and use the outhouse," Anna said. Miss Hitchcock nodded curtly and left the room.

As Anna was making her way back to the big house along the dark path, she saw two figures to her right about a dozen feet away.

"Quiet night," said one sentry.

"War's over. I expect we'll be sent out to Minnesota

to put down the Indians," a second voice said.

"Wonder if Kirkpatrick will go, now that he's found himself that wonderful mischief in the house. Ain't she somethin'? Saw her in that coach on the way up from Columbia and the fellows said they'd never seen a woman as pretty. They just stared and stared. She didn't seem to mind."

The other sentry grunted. "The colonel is sure enjoying the spoils of war, I'll say. But I'm not so sure that our beauty is a real Yankee as she says. Women, you know, have been known to spy for the Confederates. They don't raise as much dust as men spies, y'know."

Anna found the back door and silently let herself into the darkened kitchen. She saw a figure huddled on the floor. "Two?" she whispered.

"Yes," Two said, sleepily.

"It's me, Anna. I'm upstairs."

Two mumbled something that Anna didn't hear as she left the kitchen, headed for the main staircase. She saw the large figure of Col. Kirkpatrick ascending the stairs and she waited until he reached the landing. She saw that he knocked on Miss Hitchcock's door and entered.

Anna climbed the stairs as fast as she could and got into her room.

Yankees and a beautiful spy. Could it be? Anna fell asleep wondering.

Chapter Nine

Two heard the roosters crow and raised her head from the empty sack she had been sleeping on. The sun was up and she stretched and went out back to the spring house and splashed her face with the cool water. Then she crept up the front stairs to find Anna.

Two was not relaxed among these Yankees. They seemed loud and rough to her. She saw that there were a large number of her people with the soldiers in the field, working in the cook tents. She wondered what was the difference for them working for the Yankees or the Confederates. Seemed the same to her, an army. When Two got to the top of the landing she knew she was in trouble. There were a number of big, dark doors and she had no idea which one Anna was behind. If she made a mistake and knocked on the wrong one, Two thought, she would probably get a beating for leaving the kitchen. Just as she was about to turn and return downstairs, the door opposite opened and the big bulky form of Col. Kirkpatrick filled the doorway. She saw he was dressed and carried his sword. Two almost fainted from fright.

The colonel saw Two and smiled. "Your young lady is down the hall, to the right," he said, passing Two and patting her on the shoulder. Two had expected a blow. She nodded nervously and padded barefoot down the waxed wood hallway. She knocked at the door Kirkpatrick indicated and heard a sleepy, "What is it?"

"It's me, Two," Two said. Anna opened the big door and turned back to her packing.

"I wish we could stay here long enough to get our clothes washed," Anna said. "But I think we should press on."

Sergeant Caldwell found them in the main hallway. He was shaved and clean looking in a new uniform that was too large.

"Breakfast?" he called. The three walked down to a mess tent, where the soldiers made a fuss over the girls and they didn't mind that Two ate with the white folks. Two saw that two black men behind the serving counter stared at her in amazement, as if they had never seen a black girl with white folks before.

"Colonel Kirkpatrick is sending us on to Raleigh with a scouting party. We should be there this afternoon, if all goes right," Caldwell said. "I'm for it because I think I can get the cars at Raleigh and go to Wilmington and find a steamer home." Caldwell looked embarrassed.

"And, you can find your relatives in Raleigh and

connect with them until your father…" He did not finish the sentence.

"I shall be sorry to lose your company," Anna said.

"Thank you, young lady," Caldwell said. The sun warmed them as they waited. Soon they saw a commotion by the front door of the big house. Miss Hitchcock came out on the porch as a soldier drove a large, black carriage to the front door.

"Colonel Kirkpatrick wants us to ride with Miss Hitchcock on the way to Raleigh," Caldwell said, "It will be more comfortable for you."

Led by a captain, the troop moved out of the field in a column of twos, with the carriage bearing Caldwell, the girls and Miss Hitchcock bringing up the rear. She did not speak a word to any of them. Anna studied the exquisite lavender colored dress she wore and how it was buttoned from neck to waist. It fit her like a glove. Miss Hitchcock carried a furled small umbrella; Anna realized that the woman did not want to be uncomfortable in the sun.

The troop cantered down the country road, moving to the east, Anna could see by the sun. As they moved a few miles the road widened and they saw various army wagons and parties moving in the opposite direction. They came to a bridge but its bed had been torn up and the party had to slow and descend to the creek banks and slowly urge the horses across the shallow waterway. The carriage sloshed across the creek without trouble. Every once in a while Sergeant Caldwell winked at

Anna. The morning proceeded slowly and pleasantly as the troop moved eastward.

Anna saw nothing before she heard the crack, pop of the pistols and muskets from the left. Two soldiers fell from their mounts; the others skittered around, trying to determine from which direction the fire was coming. Men began yelling; and soon more men were falling from their saddles. A few dismounted and pulled their horses to the ground. They used the horses as shields. But the Yankees didn't know which direction to return fire.

When the soldier directing their carriage jumped to the ground, Caldwell took the reins and swung the vehicle around to reverse their direction.

They had gone only a few dozen yards when they saw horsemen canter from the woods, waving to them with their weapons. Caldwell raised his hands. "Unarmed!" he yelled at the men in the woods. Anna saw that they did not wear the Yankee blue but rather a mixture of butternut country garb and gray. Confederates.

The horsemen came abreast of the carriage and taking their horses' bridles, led them away, firing at the now scattered and dismounted Yankees.

Before they entered the deep woods, Anna saw a line of horsemen attack the Yankees with gunfire and sword. It was but a brief glance as the carriage moved rapidly through the underbrush. They rode for about 10 minutes, until they came to a clearing where four or five Confederate soldiers sat their horses around a little, youngish man on a small horse.

"Found these young'uns traveling with the Yankees, general," their captor told the small man.

"Children?" the small man asked. Caldwell spoke up.

"General, I'm Sergeant Caldwell, recently released from Salisbury Prison. These girls are going to Raleigh to find the father," he pointed at Anna, " of this young lady. And this is Miss Hitchcock, of ah, Columbia. We are non-combatants and expect to be treated as such. Further, the war is over."

The young bearded man looked them over, smiling slightly at Anna. She noticed that he wore a plain gray coat with a swirl of yellow piping on the cuffs. The piping made intricate loops.

"Well, let it always be said of General Wheeler that he never made war on children and non-combatants," he said. "But, you, sergeant, wear an army uniform and thus are in Federal service…"

"No, general, this uniform was given me to wear this morning because my own was in rags. I'm on my way home," Caldwell explained. The general looked to the rider who had brought the party in.

"Do we know if the party was just a skirmish line or is it part of a larger force?"

"Can't say, general. Looks like a scout party to me. They were riding down the pike like they owned it and it was a nice day for a trot. My men are engaging them now. I expect that they will fire a few rounds and then sound retreat and pull back to their encampment. Maybe they'll send out reinforcements to find and whomp us."

"Thanks, captain," Wheeler said. He turned to Anna and Caldwell. "You'll have to ride with us now. We can't afford to let you go, as you could tell the Yankees about us."

"But we don't know anything," Caldwell said. General Wheeler laughed and turned his horse away and rode out of the clearing. The captain holding their bridles followed.

Anna looked at Miss Hitchcock, who had not said a word during the entire confrontation. The young woman was nervously putting on a pair of gray gloves. She seemed more intent on being properly dressed than in being taken prisoner.

Anna wondered, too, what it meant. Now she was a prisoner of the Confederates. But she considered herself a Confederate. Her father was a Confederate. And Anna thought Miss Hitchcock was a Confederate spy. It was all too confusing. As they rode on through the woods they heard the regular crack of musket fire. The war was definitely not over.

Chapter Ten

They rode for more than an hour. Except for the fact they were in custody, it was a pleasant day. Anna thought of how quiet were her days on the farm. She was only a few days away from it and she had trouble comprehending all that had happened to her.

"What's going to happen?" Two asked nervously.

"Nothing," Miss Hitchcock said, speaking for the first time. "They'll realize that we mean no harm and they'll let us go. And, if not, well, Colonel Kirkpatrick will come find us..."

Sergeant Caldwell laughed. "You have an interesting attitude," he said. They came to a large weatherbeaten house in the woods. It was some kind of camp, Anna saw from the horses in the corral and men moving about.

"My father is with General Lee," Anna said to the captain as he dismounted. The captain smiled at her. "I have no doubt of that young lady, from your speech but it's passing strange that you are with this Yankee," he motioned to Sergeant Caldwell, who was helping Miss Hitchcock down from the carriage.

Anna saw that their arrival had stopped activity in the camp, especially when the men caught sight of Miss Hitchcock. They stood where they stopped and just stared silently. Miss Hitchcock, Anna noticed, was not at all disturbed by the attention. She accepted it as her due, Anna decided. Miss Hitchcock moved toward the old farm house and two soldiers in her path almost fell over each other getting out of her way.

The captain motioned to Anna and Caldwell to follow him. "Sergeant," the captain yelled. "Take this Negro gal to the cook tent and put her to work." A tall man with a large dark beard motioned to Two to follow him.

Anna was about to protest when she thought better of it. At least Two would get something to eat. Anna could not help but notice the difference between the Yankee and Confederate camp. The Yankees had horses to spare and plenty of equipment, such as tents. Their uniforms were new and clean. The Confederates were dressed ragtag, a mixture of what fit. Some men didn't have boots or shoes. The few horses were thin and sad looking.

The porch boards creaked as the captain, Caldwell and Anna followed Miss Hitchcock into the building. They found General Wheeler and his aides in the parlor. Wheeler was seated and the other stood. Wheeler was studying a map.

"If we can keep them from the rail line, it will buy

us time. Perhaps Davis and his party will come down from Danville on the cars. The line must be clear…"

"President Davis has already arrived in Charlotte," Anna heard herself say. The Confederate officers turned and stared at her.

"How do you know?" Wheeler asked, turning in his chair. Anna saw that he had clear blue eyes that were friendly. She was not afraid of him as she had been of Col. Kirkpatrick.

"I know because I saw him in Charlotte. We stayed at the same boarding house. He came with a party of soldiers. President Davis was in a wagon and they spoke of going south, maybe to Texas…"

"He's escaped, then," Wheeler said loudly. "Great news…"

"But the war is over," Anna added.

General Wheeler waved his right arm at Anna. "General Johnston signed a paper with Billy Sherman and those rascals in Washington refused to honor it. We are still at war…"

Anna saw that Sergeant Caldwell was about to speak but thought the better of it. She, too, didn't understand what was happening. It was all too confusing. The only one who seemed unconcerned was Miss Hitchcock. General Wheeler suddenly stood and bowed. Anna saw how small he was, not much bigger than she was. She wondered how old he was. He couldn't be that old, she thought. All the Confederate soldiers she had seen were either old or young men. General Wheeler, despite his beard, seemed a very young man.

"We are honored to have you here," Wheeler drawled at Miss Hitchcock. Anna watched as the young woman smiled.

"General," Miss Hitchcock said, "I have lived four years at Charleston and Columbia and I've never heard of our officers taking women prisoners." Anna heard the sharp edge of her voice.

"You are not my prisoner," Wheeler interrupted. "Consider yourself my guest. I do not make war on women and civilians. I am not one of those Billy Sherman bushwhacking bummers," he said emphatically. Anna saw his cheeks redden.

"You were in harm's way when we attacked that Yankee troop. We know from experience they will fight dismounted and with those repeating rifles they have the bullets fly everywhere. You were in danger."

"I demand you return us on our journey," Miss Hitchcock said. Wheeler looked away.

"I'm afraid that's not possible," he said. "Are you all hungry?" he said, changing the subject. Anna nodded.

"Youngster," Wheeler said to her, "go back out to the cook tent and tell the sergeant to bring us dinner. We'll eat here." Wheeler smiled. "I'm afraid nothing would get done out there if Miss Hitchcock ventures out."

Anna found the cook tent and told the nearest soldier what General Wheeler said. As the cook filled tin containers of beans and fatback, and garden greens to take to the house, Anna looked around for Two. She spied her stoking a fire outside a second tent. Anna walked to her.

"Did they feed you?" she asked. Two looked up, unhappy.

"They said I had to work for my dinner." Two looked around and in a lower voice, said, "They don't have the food the Yankees have."

Anna had to agree, noting the poor condition of the tenting, horses and men's clothing. The Confederacy, she saw, was ragged and thin.

The captain who had brought their carriage in said grace over the simple meal. "He's a preacher, back in Macon," Wheeler said by way of introduction. "Has his own church…"

The captain smiled at Wheeler. After the meal, Miss Hitchcock asked for a room. Wheeler showed her to the upstairs. Anna and Caldwell sat on the front porch with the captain, who pulled a brown pipe from his jacket and filled it with a wad of tan tobacco. He found a Lucifer and soon had the pipe smoking.

"Got to say the Yankees are good at making these Lucifers," the captain said.

"Are you really a preacher?" Caldwell asked.

The captain nodded. "Yes, I have Presbyterian congregation in Macon. Or, rather, I had a congregation at Macon. Been away more than two years now. Haven't had much mail from my wife these months." He laughed. "We haven't been any one place long enough to get mail, what with Sherman and Stoneman…"

"Who's Stoneman?" Caldwell asked.

The captain puffed contently on his pipe. "Stoneman is a Yankee cavalryman who brought a force over the mountains from Tennessee. Thought he could take us from the back. But General Joe," the captain motioned inside the house with his pipe, "kept Stoneman away from General Johnston. Now, if we can get this war settled right, we can return to our former lives, those of us left living."

"That's what I was intending to do, when we met this morning," Caldwell said.

"Where were you headed?" the captain asked.

Sergeant Caldwell told the captain of his capture, imprisonment at Salisbury and the events of the last few days. "All I want to do is get on a boat at Wilmington and sail home," he said softly.

"And I want to find my father," Anna interrupted. The captain looked at her.

"He'll come home, if he's able," he said. "We've heard that Lee's men have been discharged. Some have come through our lines. They," he said, "want to get home. Some are not that well. And," the captain rubbed his forehead, "we don't have any medicine for them."

At that moment Anna saw two horsemen riding hard into the yard. They dismounted and pounded into the house. The captain excused himself and joined them. Anna looked at Sergeant Caldwell.

"What are we going to do?" she asked.

He looked away and shrugged. "We could run but they might shoot. We can't risk it. Besides, we can't leave Miss Hitchcock here." Anna felt she could leave them all there but she didn't say it.

The front door opened and General Wheeler and

aides came running out to the yard.

"Get the men mounted up," Wheeler ordered the captain. "Get those wagons moving." Anna and Sergeant Caldwell stood.

General Wheeler turned and saw them for the first time. "Your Yankees are coming down the pike in force," he said. "And it looks like Kirkpatrick has joined forces with Stoneman. If not, he's got a powerful large cavalry looking for us."

There was general yelling and commotion as the soldiers saddled mounts and stowed gear. Anna and Sergeant Caldwell walked to their carriage. Two found them there. The two healthy horses that had pulled the carriage that morning were replaced by two older animals. The three settled themselves in the carriage and Sergeant Caldwell took the reins. The captain came up to them.

"I won't be able to lead you all this time but you should know we expect you to keep up with us. It would be a shame to shoot musket balls into such a fine carriage…" He smiled and Anna was not sure that he was serious.

They were almost out of the yard with the soldiers riding past when they realized that Miss Hitchcock was not with them. Sergeant Caldwell stopped the carriage and called her name. No reply. He called louder. Still no reply.

"Go get her," Sergeant Caldwell turned to Anna, who jumped down and ran into the building and up the stairs. She opened the first door she saw without knocking. Miss Hitchcock was stretched out on a straw bed covered with gray ticking.

"We're leaving," Anna said loudly. The woman on the bed did not stir. Anna moved to her side and shook her shoulder roughly. Miss Hitchcock snapped awake with a start, her blue eyes blazing with shock.

"Get up," Anna said. "The Confederates are moving. We have to go with them." Anna ran from the room and heard Miss Hitchcock moving behind her. Anna leaped into the carriage as Miss Hitchcock made her way down the inside stairs. "She's coming," Anna said.

When the young woman settled herself in the carriage, Sergeant Caldwell flicked the reins and the old horses moved out, trying to catch the other mounts they had been with this campaign.

"Why are we leaving? We just arrived…" Miss Hitchcock asked Sergeant Caldwell. He turned in his seat and said, "Col. Kirkpatrick's cavalry is on the pike. He probably learned of the ambush this morning and your capture and he's out to slam General Wheeler for it. Let's pray we can outrun him…"

"Why?" Anna cried.

"Because," Sergeant Caldwell said, "if Kirkpatrick and Wheeler meet up there will be a major battle and we'll be in the middle of it. And, neither one gives a damn that the war is over." Anna saw that Sergeant Caldwell made a sour face.

They rode more than an hour as the sun began its slide to dusk. They moved on a country road, away from the pike. It meandered across fields, streams, dells and farm land. Wheeler's men moved fast and quietly. Anna decided the Yankees made more noise on the march. The Confederates had less equipment thus less noise. Their horses seemed to know what to do without much direction. The party moved at a steady trot. At one point General Wheeler came riding back the line to the carriage. He turned and spoke to its passengers.

"We're headed for Joe Johnston's camp but I'm not sure we'll find it before dark. If not, we'll make a quick camp and join up tomorrow. " He paused. "My scouts say Kirkpatrick's people are looking for us on the other side of the pike. They're wasting time but it will soon occur to them we're not there and then the hound will chase the hare…"

They did not find General Johnston before dusk and General Wheeler called a halt near a large field. He motioned for his troopers to move to the tree line a few hundred yards away. The soldiers rode to the trees and quietly dismounted and began making overnight camp. The trees and underbrush were too thick for Sergeant Caldwell to pull the carriage beyond the tree line. It would be visible from the road. Nothing to be done about it.

Sergeant Caldwell turned to Anna. "You and Two, go gather some firewood and we'll make a meal, if we can borrow from these people."

Anna and Two returned with arm loads of dry wood and found General Wheeler at the carriage. He said to Sergeant Caldwell, "No fires. Cold camp. Don't want any smoke telling Yankees where we are."

Anna at that moment had a cold feeling that the Yankees knew where they were, fire or no fire.

Chapter Eleven

Two awoke at first light. It was dark under the carriage where she had crawled to sleep. She was chilled and the grass was slippery with dew. She looked through the spokes of the nearest wheel and saw Sergeant Caldwell curled asleep. Anna and Miss Hitchcock shared the carriage seats.

Something had awakened Two and she couldn't decide what it was. She crawled out from under the carriage and stared across the field. All was silent. Behind the line of trees Two knew the Confederate soldiers slept. She could make out the shadows of one or two that were on guard duty. Then Two recognized what had awakened her. The woods were too silent. It was near dawn and there were no birds chirping or other wood animal sounds. The rising sun threw long shadows, enabling Two to see a nearby fence line. She walked to it and down to the road.

That was when she saw them, two mounted soldiers. Yankees, she thought, from their dark uniforms. She stopped, frightened that they had seen her. The cavalrymen sat their big horses easy, with carbines resting in their laps. Two knew that soon the sun would put her in profile to the men. She fell silently to the ground.

"What do you make of it?" one soldier asked the other.

"Looks like her carriage," the second said. "Kirkpatrick described it well enough. Should be rebs around, f'sure."

At his last word a shot was fired, and one horse scampered in a tight circle. Two heard a piercing whistle behind her. The Confederates had seen the Yankees. She hugged the ground, praying that the Yankees had not seen her. Another shot and the two Federal cavalrymen turned their horses and galloped back down the road. Two stood and ran as fast as she could to the carriage. Anna was awake, her head peering over the black door. Miss Hitchcock, Two saw, was up and trying to tie on her hat. She seemed unconcerned by the gunfire.

Sergeant Caldwell came around the carriage. "What was it?" he asked Two.

She pointed down the road. "Yankees, two of 'em, come up the road. I heard them. They saw the carriage…"

"Oh, my," Anna said.

At that moment the entire woods erupted in activity as the Confederates struck their cold camp. A low muttering was heard from the tree line and soon General Wheeler appeared on horseback.

"My men say there were two Yankee pickets out.

Probably from Kirkpatrick. Looking for Miss Hitchcock, I assume."

Sergeant Caldwell stepped forward. "More the reason to let us go," he said.

"Well, they know where we are now and there's no gettin' by that," Wheeler replied.

"I don't think it matters what I do with you folks now. In a while there's gonna be a pile of Yankees come down that road and we'll be here to meet 'em. Trouble is, there're more of them than us. I don't think you can outrun them."

Anna saw Sergeant Caldwell's shoulders sag. The rising sun warmed them but Anna knew it would further expose them to Kirkpatrick's force. Soon they heard bugles. General Wheeler turned his horse and galloped back to the tree line.

"Get down out of the carriage and under it," Sergeant Caldwell ordered. Anna jumped down.

"I'm not going to mess my clothes under this thing," Miss Hitchcock said. Sergeant Caldwell could only stare at her. Before he could reply there was commotion on the road and they saw troops of blue-clad riders, bright flags flapping in the morning breeze, arrive on the road. It was a glorious sight, Anna thought before realizing that there would be a battle and that they were in the middle of it. They had no escape. There were no horses for the carriage and it seemed senseless to run for it. Someone was bound to shoot them.

Caldwell, Two and Anna fell to the grass under the

carriage and watched as the Yankees stopped on the road and formed columns left, with officers shouting commands. Bugles and voices filled the field. The Confederates were silent. Anna wondered what General Wheeler would do. Would he ride into the massed Yankees. That didn't seem the wise course. Suddenly, Anna and the others saw Col. Kirkpatrick in the midst of the formation. He was pointing at them, at the carriage. At the same time his men were dismounting and taking prone positions and kneeling ranks, with their short-barrel carbines gleaming in the sun. Anna, smelling the fresh grass beneath her, wondered if she would see the end of the day or her parents again. All this before breakfast, she thought as her stomach growled. She realized she had not eaten much the day before. She was hungry. Well, there was nothing to do for it.

Suddenly, Sergeant Caldwell slid out from under the carriage and was up on his feet before Anna could respond. She saw his drawn, thin face was gray with fatigue. Before she could utter a word, Sergeant Caldwell began walking toward the Yankees. When he was a hundred yards from the carriage, he began waving his arms.

"Don't shoot," he yelled. "We are all right. Don't shoot!" Anna could see the ranks of Yankees move as the soldiers looked to their officers for orders.

"Dear God!" Anna heard Miss Hitchcock say from above. "Come back," she screamed.

Sergeant Caldwell reached mid-field, about 100

yards from the nearest Yankee when they heard Col. Kirkpatrick yell, "Hold fire, hold fire. Let him come in…"

Sergeant Caldwell lowered his arms and began walking rapidly toward the Yankee line when Anna heard the single shot and saw the puff as the bullet struck Sergeant Caldwell's jacket. He fell face forward without a sound.

"No!" Anna screamed and involuntarily scrambled out from under the carriage. Two was with her and without thinking they began to run to the fallen soldier.

The sight of two girls, one white, one black, running across the field, surprised the cavalrymen. "Hold fire, hold fire," Kirkpatrick yelled again, his horse prancing in circles in the midst of his men.

When Anna and Two reached Sergeant Caldwell they were out of breath, sobbing from the run and anger that their friend had been shot. They stared at his body. Hot tears rolled from their eyes. Anna didn't know what to do—here it was a beautiful morning and they were in the middle of a battle whose first casualty was their friend. Anna had seen dead people before and she said a short, silent prayer that Sergeant Caldwell was not dead. As if to answer her, he groaned. She saw that the bullet had cut a large, round hole in his jacket and it was filled with blood.

Anna turned, as for help from any quarter and as she did she saw the Confederates emerge from the tree line on foot, ranks holding long-barrel muskets at the ready. The two girls were on the killing ground.

Chapter Twelve

Anna heard Two's keening sound, a loud scream. Anna decided to scream, too. What else could she do? The two girls circled each other, screaming in frustration that they were between two forces determined to kill each other.

Accidently, they stood back to back. Anna faced the Confederates and Two faced the Yankees.

It saved their lives. The Confederates saw the tall, blonde white girl screaming at them and the Yankees saw Two, the black girl, waving her arms and sobbing.

They both felt it was only a matter of moments before the field would rock with the sound of guns and bullets would spin like angry bees to their targets. Surprisingly, Anna had no fear of death. She was driven by anger that Sergeant Caldwell had been shot, that she couldn't stop the coming clash of arms. Out of the corner of her eye, Anna saw Miss Hitchcock standing in the carriage, her right hand holding a handkerchief to her mouth.

The opposing forces seemed unwilling to make the first move and thus the standoff gave them all a chance to hear the approaching bugle calls. Anna turned her head and saw a small party of Yankees on horseback, galloping down the road. Two soldiers rode ahead, she saw, carrying large white flags, and two of the horsemen wore Confederate gray. The soldiers with the white flags quickly rode to mid-field near the girls and waved the white flags. Anna saw the rest of the party approach Col. Kirkpatrick and soon the two Confederate officers rode slowly into the field and toward General Wheeler. As they rode past her, Anna saw a tired looking, gray bearded man in a soiled uniform with lots of yellow striping on the arms of his coat, accompanied by a younger officer.

With her breathing coming in gasps, Anna could see the Confederate officers stop near Wheeler. The older man removed his wide-brim hat and began speaking. Wheeler listened and then slowly lowered his sword to salute the older man.

"Stand down, stand down," General Wheeler yelled. His men lowered their muskets. "Stack arms," he commanded. The ragtag soldiers began the process of making standing pyramids of every three weapons. Anna turned to see the Yankee troopers lowering their carbines and moving back to their horses.

Anna realized that there would be no killing. She screamed again and hugged Two. They danced around the fallen body of Sergeant Caldwell. The two soldiers bearing the white flags came up to them. One turned to the second, "Get some stretcher bearers," he ordered. The second man ran off. Soon two other soldiers ran to where they stood and quickly placed Sergeant Caldwell on the stretcher and carried him toward the road. Anna and Two followed silently.

At the road they were surrounded by Yankee soldiers, some of them smiling widely. Soon a cheer rose from the troops and some tossed their caps in the air. "It's over," one soldier yelled. The group parted for the mounted group. Anna saw it was Col. Kirkpatrick and a smaller, red-haired man in a plain blue coat with gold shoulder straps that had stars on them.

"General Sherman," Col. Kirkpatrick said, "may I present Miss Anna Williams. She kept us from a terrible mistake here this morning."

Anna was stunned. She was facing the devil himself, the general who had ripped the Confederacy from one end to the other. He looked like a peddler she had once seen at the Lincoln County courthouse. His red hair stuck out in all directions and his red beard made him look fierce. Anna saw that his eyes, however, were smiling.

"How old are you" General Sherman asked Anna. She told him.

"I have a daughter back in Ohio about your age. I sure wouldn't want her on this battlefield," he said in a surprisingly soft voice.

Anna stood straighter. "I'm on my way to find my father. He is with General Lee."

Sherman shot a look at Col. Kirkpatrick. "Colonel,

I would take it as a personal favor if you would help this young lady find her father. I think she did us all a favor this morning by stopping further bloodshed." With that Sherman raised his gloved right hand and saluted Kirkpatrick and moved away.

Anna looked at Kirkpatrick. "We're hungry," she said. The colonel laughed, spun his horse and barked orders. Soon men were running, carrying tins of prepared stew. Anna and Two sat by the side of the road and ate with tin spoons. The food, Anna decided, was a gift from the heavens. When she was finished, Anna turned and stared across the field toward where the Confederate soldiers sat dejectedly around their stacked arms as Confederate and Yankee officers walked among them. Anna wandered close and heard them explaining the final surrender terms that General Sherman had worked with General Johnston.

Suddenly, Anna felt a wave of guilt wash over her. She was thinking of herself when Sergeant Caldwell was probably dying of his bullet wound.

Anna found Col. Kirkpatrick dismounted nearby and asked for the sergeant. The colonel motioned to a young officer. "Take her to him," he commanded. The officer found a horse for Anna and Two and they galloped down the road toward the pike. Anna prayed they would be in time.

Chapter Thirteen

The horse bearing Anna and Two cantered easily behind the young lieutenant. They headed west for about a mile and then south to the Raleigh pike. Where the country road joined the pike, they found a mass of soldiers, wagons and tents. The army was setting up camp.

The lieutenant asked for the medical area and was directed to a large tent by the roadside, where they dismounted. A large sergeant stopped them from entering the tent. "Can't go in there," he said.

"I'm under orders from Col. Kirkpatrick. And he," the lieutenant raised his voice, "is under orders from General Sherman." The sergeant stepped aside. At first Anna was momentarily blinded by the tent's darkness after the glare of the day. She heard the buzz of flies. They saw two men in dark coats at the rear of the tent, bending over a figure on a stretcher. It was Sergeant Caldwell. His uniform jacket had been removed and Anna could see a clean, white bandage had been applied to his chest where the bullet had exited.

The lieutenant explained their presence to the two men in black who introduced themselves as contract surgeons. Anna didn't know what the term meant.

"His wound is pretty clean and from the bleeding it doesn't appear the round hit an artery," one of the surgeons said. "The round went clear through, which is good. We've given him some laudanum to make him sleep. All we can do now is watch him."

Anna looked at Sergeant Caldwell and was frightened. He was so still she thought he was dead.

"We would like to stay with him," Anna said. The surgeons looked at one another. "General Sherman's orders," the lieutenant said. He turned and saluted Anna. "I'll be back later to see how you are," he said, leaving the tent.

"Well, I guess you two can stay over here," one surgeon said, pointing to a large chest near a heavy wood table that was stained dark red. Anna did not want to ask what had made the stain. She was afraid to learn the answer.

"We'll be in the next tent," the surgeon said. "They've just brought some Rebs in and we're to look at them."

Anna and Two sat on the large chest and stared at Sergeant Caldwell. He lay on his back and his breathing was soft. After awhile he gave a soft moan and began to move. They ran to him.

Sergeant Caldwell opened his eyes. "What….?"

"You were shot," Anna said, bending over his face.

"Thirsty…" he said, running his tongue over his lips. Anna looked around for a canteen. There was none. She ran outside to where the sergeant was seated at a folding chair and table.

"Water. He wants water," she said. The sergeant nodded to a nearby tree. "Take one of 'em canteens over there." Anna saw three army canteens hanging in the shade. She ran and took one and returned to Sergeant Caldwell's side. Two was kneeling at his side, staring at his face. Sergeant Caldwell tried to smile at her.

Anna kneeled and unscrewed the tin canteen top. She prayed that the water was clean as she raised Sergeant Caldwell's head to sip.

He took the water greedily. She poured only a small amount to his mouth. Anna looked around and said to Two. "Find a switch and keep these flies out of here." Two ran out of the tent and returned in a few minutes with an evergreen switch and used it to swat the flies that were congregating in the tent.

All afternoon Anna let Sergeant Caldwell sip from the canteen. At one point she said to Two, "Go find some food." The black girl ran from the tent and returned later with a tin plate bearing a sizzling beef steak from the fire.

"Get me a clean knife," Anna commanded. Two went to the sergeant outside the tent and returned with a large military-style knife. Anna tested its blade and found it sharp. She cut the beef into small pieces and holding Sergeant Caldwell's head up, she used the knife point to spear small pieces of the meat and place them on his lips. Surprisingly, Sergeant Caldwell was able to chew and swallow the meat. Its juice ran down his chin. Anna wiped it away with the hem of her skirt. After he ate, Sergeant Caldwell sank back on the stretcher and groaned again before falling asleep, his head turned to the right. Anna saw a blue blanket folded on a nearby chest and opened it over his form.

Anna and Two retreated to sit on the big chest.

"It's been an amazing day," Anna said to her companion.

"We almost got shot," Two said.

Anna smiled. "You went out there on that field with me. You didn't have to do that. You're free now. You can do what you want."

"I went out there because you were there. You are my friend," Two said.

Anna hugged Two. "Thank God this war is over and we can get back to Mama and Settie One. They will be so happy to see father." Anna was silent for a moment.

"Will you and Settie One want to return to the farm with us?" Anna asked. Settie Two looked at the other girl without responding for some moments.

"The Yankees say we are free and now we can have new lives. I don't know what that means. I think we would be happy with those people we know, rather than with strangers. And, this world is big and strange. I think I want to return to the place I know. With you. If freedom means I can pick now, I pick you."

Anna hugged Two again and the girls laughed. The

afternoon was warm and soon the pair were dozing, their bodies resting against each other.

Anna awakened with a start noticing a figure at the tent flap and the dusk beyond. The figure came toward them. Anna was surprised to see that it was the Confederate captain who had taken them prisoner.

He smiled down at them. "Now that it's over, I can return to my former profession and minister where needed," he said. "How is your friend?"

"Sleeping," Anna said, pointing to Sergeant Caldwell. "We fed him some beef and water." The captain went to the sleeping figure and knelt beside him, feeling the pulse in his neck and checking the bandage. Anna knelt beside him.

"Will he live?" she asked.

The captain looked at her and smiled. "With an angel of mercy as you watching over him, he should." Anna reddened with embarrassment.

The captain stood wearily. "Now I must return to our men. We have lots of invalids the Yankees have collected outside. They are returning from Virginia and many have collapsed with the fever. The Yankees are putting up more tents and will quarantine them."

"From Virginia?" Anna asked, her heart thumping.

"Yes," the captain said, moving toward the tent entrance. She followed him to where the soldiers in blue were pounding stakes for more tents. Gray-clad figures rested against trees; some were stretched out on the ground without cover.

Anna went among them, staring at the dirt-stained

thin faces. Most seemed unaware of their surroundings.

"Is anyone here from the Fourth North Carolina," Anna asked repeatedly and desperately. A dozen ghostly figures only stared at her without replying. One man, dressed in colorless rags and barefoot, aimlessly moved his right arm in an up and down motion. He seemed unaware he was doing this.

"North Carolinians to the front," this scarecrow suddenly yelled. The arm motion continued. Anna moved among the men as the dusk cast long shadows and made them hard to see. She repeated the name of her father and his regiment. She had about canvassed the sick and injured men without response when one bearded man resting against a tree trunk, repeated her father's name. Twice.

Chapter Fourteen

Anna went close to the bearded man whose face was smoke-and-dirt-stained. He was almost unconscious. He repeated her father's name.

"Father?" Anna cried, reaching out for his shoulder. He didn't look like the man who had left their farm to go to General Lee. The man muttered the name of the regiment and waved a limp arm toward some wagons nearby.

"Over there," he said. Anna rushed to the open wagon and saw it contained four gray-clad soldiers lying on the wagon bed. They were shoeless and looked like scarecrows wearing rags over their thin bodies. Anna climbed up on a wheel and called her father's name.

"Here," a weak voice replied. Her heart leapt.

"Father," she screamed, climbing into the wagon to clutch the figure who half raised himself. She saw it was her father, much thinner and with a longer dirtier beard. Hot tears filled Anna's eyes and she was unable to see. She stopped, afraid she would stumble on these sick men.

At that moment she heard the faint sounds of lively music and looked for its origin. By the pike she saw a commotion and heard yelling. Soldiers were tossing their caps in the air as a party on horseback arrived. Two soldiers carried bright flags, small flags with stars on them. She recognized General Sherman. His group moved to the side of the road as a marching band took position in the road and played a tune. She had never heard such music before. She turned to her father but he had slid down on the wagon bed. He reached up his right hand and clutched her arm. She smiled at him and saw tears in his eyes. "Anna," he said.

Anna didn't realize she was still standing in the wagon bed until she heard a horse canter up. It was General Sherman, followed by the soldiers with the flags and others.

"Well, Miss, are you all right?" Sherman asked in a gruff voice. Anna knew he sounded angry but wasn't.

"Yes, I've just found my father, thank the Lord." she replied.

"Thank the Lord," Sherman said, peering over the wagon side to the men inside. Sherman turned in his saddle and said to an assistant. "I want these men in tents tonight. Same care we give our own. Bring up our own army doctors. It's time for healing, time for healing," he muttered. The assistant saluted and rode back to the road and quickly a company was formed and marched to erect more tents for the sick.

"Could I move my father into the tent with Sergeant Caldwell?" Anna asked Sherman.

Before he could answer, one of the black-coat contract surgeons spoke, "We don't put Rebels with our men, general."

Sherman looked down at Anna. "The war is over, sir. Put this man where this young lady wants. I will be back to see them both." Sherman turned in his saddle. "I want these men to share our rations for as long as they are with us. Without exception," he snapped. The group of officers behind him nodded.

Two soldiers with a stretcher carried Anna's father to the tent and placed him near Sergeant Caldwell. Anna found a basin, water and soap and began to wash her father's face, neck and hands.

Two came with a fresh canteen and Anna put it to her father's lips and he drank. She felt his face was feverish but at least clean. She could do nothing about the rags he wore tied with a leather belt. The Yankee sergeant entered the tent with two oil lamps, which he placed on the trunk and the lamps gave Anna and Two enough light to minister to the fallen men. Two went for food and returned with two tins of stew. They fed Sergeant Caldwell and Mr. Williams. The girls shared one tin. Anna turned to Two. "We found him," she said, beaming. At that moment a young officer carrying a black bag entered the tent and went to the men on the stretchers.

"These must be the men the general asked us to look at," he said to the girls. He pulled the blanket back from Sergeant Caldwell and removed the bandage slowly. Part of it stuck to the wound. Anna and Two watched as the officer took a bottle from his bag and with a clean bandage began to clean the wound area. He felt the sergeant's pulse as the sleeping man came awake, starting at the stranger above him.

"I'm Doctor Logan," the officer said. "Your wound looks clean. We may have to cauterize it tomorrow." Anna did not know what that meant, but it sounded serious. The sergeant nodded.

"Do you have pain?" the doctor asked.

Sergeant Caldwell nodded again. The doctor took another bottle from the bag, opened its top and held it to the sergeant's lips. "More laudanum. It'll make you sleep."

When he was finished with the sergeant the doctor moved to Mr. Williams, first smiling at the girls. Anna saw that he was young and clean shaven, unusual among the bearded soldiers and their generals.

The doctor kneeled in front of Mr. Williams and studied him. He placed his hand on Mr. Williams' forehead. He opened the man's tattered shirt and inspected his narrow chest.

"Can you sit up?" he asked. Mr. Williams struggled and with the doctor's help managed to get to a sitting position on the stretcher.

"Have you eaten?" the doctor asked. Mr. Williams nodded and smiled for the first time, turning his head toward his daughter.

"Came down with a fever…on the road…paroled to return home…" Anna's father said with great effort. The doctor helped the patient to lie down.

"Sergeant," the doctor called. The Yankee sergeant entered the tent. "Find some men to stay here in this tent all night. I want this man's clothing changed. Put him in one of our uniforms, if necessary. Something clean. I want him fed every two hours and at the same time give him water. Plenty of water. Wake me if there is any change in either one. Is that understood?"

"Yes, sir," the sergeant said. "The girls…."

"Will stay here, if they choose," the doctor said, smiling again in their direction. "It seems they have a friend in General Billy and you know how he gets if someone disregards his orders." The Yankee sergeant did not reply but left the tent. Soon he returned with another soldier and they carefully removed the rags from Mr. Williams.

Anna and Two slid down the trunk on which they had sat and soon their heads touched and they slipped into sleep.

At one point in the night Anna awakened to the sound of rain on the tent. Then she fell asleep to its comforting sound.

Anna awoke to the smell of coffee, rich and grand. She was hungry. Doctor Logan was examining Sergeant Caldwell. Through the open tent flap, Anna saw the storm clouds of the night pushed east by the strong wind. It would be a clear day.

She went to her father, who was dressed now in a simple blue jacket and trousers provided by the Yankees. She saw that his beard contained white, as did his hair.

If she had passed him on the road, she thought, she would not have recognized him. The thought made her shudder. As if he knew she was by, he awoke and tried to sit up on his stretcher. The soldier orderlies came into the tent with pails of stew and coffee. She helped her father eat, after which Mr. Williams groaned and slid down. He clutched his stomach.

"Can't eat too much. Small amounts," the orderly said.

Anna went to Sergeant Caldwell's side, where Dr. Logan was putting a new bandage on the wound. The doctor looked at Anna and said, "Wound seems clean. Don't think I'll have to cauterize it…"

"What does that mean?" she asked.

"Ah, put a hot brand on it," he said. Anna winced.

Sergeant Caldwell seemed awake but groggy. "The laudanum is making him sleepy and that's to the good," the doctor said. Sergeant Caldwell tried to smile at Anna.

The day passed quickly with Anna and Two caring for the two men. Occasionally, Anna left the tent and saw that the camp had grown as soldiers arrived from the east and west, mostly on foot. She saw the line of tents expand and heard the bark of orders. She saw, too, that the soldiers had set up more tents for the invalids, as General Sherman had ordered. Some had crude wood signs on the tent poles, reading "Quarantine."

"The men have fevers," Dr. Logan said when she asked about that. "They cannot be allowed to spread it to the army."

Anna saw, too, that beside some of the tents were covered figures on stretchers on the ground. "We lost them during the night," the doctor explained. "They will be buried here." Anna and Two watched as soldiers dug a trench and placed the bodies in it and covered them with dirt.

During the afternoon, Anna and Two went to the pike road to hear the military band tunes. They were surprised to see small drummer boys, younger than they, leading the bands, marching proudly among the Yankees.

They saw a group of men marching in ragged order from the east. They were dressed in the ragged remains of Confederate uniform—butternut homespun trousers and shirts and carrying canteens and simple packs. The Yankees began to hoot and jeer the Confederates. Soon Col. Kirkpatrick's booming voice was heard, commanding the soldiers to be quiet and step back from the road. He ordered the Yankees to ranks as the Confederate parolees marched past. Anna saw that many were shoeless. They walked in a relaxed loping walk, as if out for a day's hunting. Some carried their belongings on crude poles strung between shoulders, front to back. None were armed. At the rear of this ragtag regiment, a few officers rode thin, tired horses. One wearing a pair of elegant gray gloves gave a smart salute to Col. Kirkpatrick as he passed the Yankee formation. The band struck up "Dixie," and the Yankee soldiers sang the refrain loudly.

Col. Kirkpatrick spied Anna and directed his horse to her side. "Well, young lady, you really had the angels on your side yesterday…" He was smiling.

"Yes," Anna said, "I've found my father and now I have to get him to Charlotte Town. My mother…" Anna found she was unable to finish the thought.

"Some of my men are going there to disarm General Hoge's men. Perhaps we can provide an escort. We need to rebuild the rail line as well.

"Thank you, colonel," Anna said. "Is Miss Hitch-cock well?"

"Yes, indeedy," the big Yankee said, a wide smile changing his face. "She survived yesterday with no ill effects, save nerves from fear that you would be killed out there on that field by yourself. She is going under escort to Raleigh and from there to Wilmington and by boat to Philadelphia. We shall be married there."

Col. Kirkpatrick looked at Two. "And, will you be joining the young lady back at Charlotte?" Two nodded.

"You know you are free, don't you. You don't have to go if you don't want. No one can force you to do that," Kirkpatrick said.

"My mama is at Charlotte," Two said. "She will want to hear the adventure we have had. She'll believe me if Anna is there to tell her, too." Anna smiled at her companion.

"At your service," Col. Kirkpatrick saluted Anna.

Two days later Anna and Two climbed into a wagon where orderlies had already placed Mr. Williams. He was stronger and able to travel. He sat and clutched Anna's hand.

Anna had said good-bye to Sergeant Caldwell in the tent. He was still sleeping much of the time, though Dr. Logan said he was coming along fine.

"The wound is healing and I don't think there's much damage. His breathing is better so I think the bullet did not damage his lung. When he can be moved we'll take him to the hospital in Raleigh. He should be able to make it home."

Anna looked down at the sleeping Yankee and took his left hand and squeezed it. It wasn't much of a farewell but she hadn't expected to feel such fondness for a Yankee.

The April adventure was over and they were all going home. Perhaps tomorrow would bring more adventures.

April Adventure was designed by Tom Suzuki, Tom Suzuki, Inc., Falls Church, Virginia. The cover design is also by Tom Suzuki. The book was printed by Lightning Print Inc., La Vergne, Tennessee.

The text is 12.5 on 15 Adobe Garamond, the display type is Poetica Chancery.